FLOOD. RINSE. DRAIN. REPEAT.

And Fifty-One Other Short Stories

SUDEEPA NAIR

INDIA • SINGAPORE • MALAYSIA

ISBN 979-8-89475-969-2

CONTENTS

A NOTE

Short stories force us to examine the microcosm of life, to focus our lens onto a character, a specific existence, and a unique perspective.

An anthology of short stories offers tiny samplers at a single place like a mezze or a dessert platter.

While there was no particular theme when I began, a pattern has emerged from the stories I wrote. The choice of themes closely resembles the cyclical nature of life, seasons, nature, and even our internal monologues.

Our reactions and responses to incidents in life often follow the cycle of Flood, Rinse, Drain, and Repeat.

Emotions, happiness, sadness, exhilaration, sorrow, fears, jubilation, pride, and embarrassment flood our lives unannounced, rinse residual feelings from the previous floods, drain away on their own, and then repeat. It was a similar experience as I indulged in writing experiments every week.

The stories are spread across genres and are of varying lengths. They are set from the early 1990s to the present; some are imagined in the future. (Thanks to my love for science fiction!)

My characters live in the cities and villages, but I draw heavily from my early life in Mumbai and migrant experiences across international cities. I hope you enjoy the variety.

The last three stories stand apart as character sketches. If you have read my latest novel, Jomo Calls, you will get more insights into the three main characters. If you haven't read the book, I hope the stories inspire you to pick it up.

INNOCENCE

"The most potent muse of all is our inner child."

– Stephen Nachmanovitch

A LUNCH TALE

The steel lunch box gleamed on the kitchen counter. Eight-year-old Sreya stood beside it, breathing in deeply. She loved the aroma when the box was opened. But she had to wait for two more hours.

"Stop sniffing around like a puppy, Sreya," her grandmother remarked. "You look famished. Shall I serve you rice?"

Sreya shook her head and ran outside. The street was empty. It will be full of dancing feet and chattering tongues in a while. The secondary classes will be dismissed soon.

Sreya skipped around, wondering what she could do until then. Her grandmother had followed her outside. "Don't play in the afternoon sun, Sreya. Come back inside and eat something. Lunch can't be four biscuits."

"I'll eat later."

Grandmother shook her head. "If your parents had been home, you wouldn't do this."

Sreya came skipping inside. She propped her head up on her grandmother's lap. "Why aren't they at home?" Her bright, mischievous eyes looked innocently at grandmother's wizened face.

"What kind of a question is this? Naughty girl. You know they have to work."

Sreya giggled and hopped back outside. She sat at the doorstep, balancing her round face on her two tiny palms, two pigtails dangling on either side. She strained her ears for laughter and squinted her eyes to look for swinging school bags. No, they were not here yet.

Sreya skipped back in to get some chalks— white, blue, pink, and yellow— and she picked them all.

Squatting down at the doorstep, she drew tiny flowers on the paved pathway. Once she covered the space in front of her door, she kept moving and drawing till she reached the next door. A padlock dangled on it. Aunty won't be back until late in the night.

Sreya poked her nose in through the dusty grill. The smell was intoxicating. She drew a deep breath and immediately started sneezing. Walking back to her door, Sreya rubbed her tummy. Hunger growled back at her. She trooped inside quietly and drank a glass of water.

"Sreya?" asked her grandmother, who dozed on a chair. "Is it time for your lunch?"

"No, Ammamma, I am not hungry."

Sreya went back to her perch at the doorstep. Her tummy was now quiet, but her thoughts returned to the gleaming lunch box on the kitchen platform. She looked longingly at the end of the street. The first group of students should be walking in any time now. Sreya gazed at the Jamun tree across the street. The branches swayed in the afternoon breeze. Before long, she curled up on the doorstep and went to sleep. Until someone grazed her cheek. "Sreya?"

Sreya opened her eyes to see a sweaty, mud-streaked face. "Gunnu Dada!" She jumped up and down and shouted in excitement. "Ammamma, Gunnu Dada is here! I am hungry!"

Gunnu smacked his lips in anticipation. He went inside, cleaned up, and took the lunch box from the kitchen platform. Sreya's grandmother took out two plates. In one, she served rotis and moth-bean curry from the lunch box. In the other, she served rice and sambhar from her kitchen. She then placed the rotis in front of Gunnu and the rice in front of Sreya. They both looked at her. She sighed. Then, she exchanged the plates. Gunnu and Sreya grinned as they devoured their favourite food.

"Gunnu, how many times have I told your mother not to send the lunch box for you. There's no need to make two lunches. You stay next door but eat here every day."

Gunnu grinned in reply. Sreya cackled with happiness.

THE TREASURE ROOM

The household slept soundly on a quiet winter night. Timid Mini gathered all her courage, as much as a ten-year-old could garner, and tiptoed out of the room.

Despite the December nip, her parents kept the bedroom door open to let the breeze flow. The tiny, archaic rooms in their ancestral home had only one window. It was an architecture suited for tropical climes and simpler times without global warming.

Mini rubbed her nervous, moisture-laden hands. She was on a mission to cross over from the room she shared with her parents to the other end of the corridor, where they held the family treasures.

It was a well-planned expedition, but she got jittery as she reached Uncle Pal's bedroom. Going past his door was the most challenging part. She wasn't afraid of the dark, the night creatures, or the grandfather clock, even though she jumped out of her skin when it struck eleven. She was terrified of grumpy Uncle Pal, who guarded their family treasures with an iron hand. The sour face, grumpy grunts, and ice-cold stares occasionally pierced by a booming voice scared her the most. But she decided that this year's vacation would be worthwhile. She will lay her hands on the treasure.

Mini brushed past the rocking chair that stood by a window close to Uncle Pal's bedroom. It swayed gently on its curved legs. Mini caught her breath. To the family, the chair symbolised Uncle Pal. One never disturbed it, just like you never upset Uncle Pal. Children making noise on the lawn outside, plucking mangoes from the orchard, vehicles honking outside the gate, vendors peddling their wares—nuisance came in various forms to annoy Uncle Pal. One must be as quiet as a mouse when he was around.

Can she reach her target without creating a ruckus?

All her recurrent thoughts vanished as she approached the treasure room. She pushed the door, which was ajar, and gasped. At the far end of the room, on an armchair, sat Uncle Pal. He was dozing. Mini was in a fix.

Should she turn around and run? Or quickly steal from the riches displayed on the floor-to-ceiling shelves in the room?

Uncle Pal moved his head, and Mini lost her courage. She stepped back quietly, walking backward to the door. The book in his hand fell, and he woke up.

“What? What are you doing here?” His voice sounded normal, unlike the boom she occasionally encountered around the house. She pointed to a section on the shelf.

Uncle Pal smiled. He motioned her to come forward and take what she wanted.

Mini’s eyes opened wide in excitement. She pounced upon a colourful spine and was about to run away when Uncle Pal said, “The library is the best spot to read in the entire house. Come sit here.” He pointed to a chair in the other corner and switched on the lamp beside it.

Timid Mini and grumpy Uncle Pal settled for a wonderful night of reading and imagining.

That night, the room turned from a closely guarded treasure to a generous bequest.

THE AFTERNOON PHOTOGRAPHER

Nisha's heart pounded as she opened the camera pouch. She ran her fingers over the grainy black texture of its body even as she snuggled it tight in her arms. If it fell, there would be no end to her guilt.

She tip-toed to her parent's bedroom. Their rhythmic snores reached her ears through a chink in the door. She slinked back, never losing her grip on the camera. It was only a week old in the family. Dad explained how the new camera makes photography a child's play. "Just aim and click," he said. Nisha listened carefully. Her round eyes captured the tiniest actions performed by her dad's fingers as he took it out of its pouch, aimed it at their couch, and clicked.

A nature lover, Dad stepped out to shoot the trees, mangoes, guavas, and even shrubs. Which is when Nisha got this idea. She had something to prove to her friends. Her classmates wouldn't believe it when she told them about her neighbour.

"Impossible!"

"You are lying!"

"Perhaps you saw it in a movie!"

She was out to prove that this timid, shy eleven-year-old knew her neighbourhood residents well. She stepped out into their yard and walked into the shrubs. The neighbour was punctual and loved the afternoon sun. Soon, the birds chirped louder, and Nisha aimed her camera. There he comes!

Point and click. So easy!

She nearly dropped her camera as she skipped home in happiness. It remained untouched for another week until the family had a wedding.

Dad scoffed at the official photographers and shot several candid ones. "Natural photography," he said, patting his new possession.

A week later, there was a heated discussion about one of the invitees. "Did he attend or not?" He was not in the wedding album.

"Check in the ones you clicked," Mom ordered Dad.

Dad rolled his eyes.

"This is important. We need to know!"

"Ok!" Dad got the photographs printed at a nearby studio.

"Here. Enjoy your treasure hunt," he said as he handed the bunch to Mom.

Mom spent a happy hour reviewing the photographs, reliving the joyous family reunion, remembering the odd jokes, the gossip, and the compliments. "My saree looks good," she said with a smile. "It's a pity that you aren't visible anywhere." She threw a withering look at Dad.

"I was the photographer."

Mom reached the last of the prints and then gasped. “Is this the first photo you took with this camera? How horrible? You could have clicked mine. Or Nisha’s? And we have this dangerous creature living in our midst?” She shuddered as she lifted her legs instinctively.

Dad craned his neck. “What is it?” His eyes lit up when he saw the picture.

“Beautiful photography, the right light, and exposure.” He beamed and then frowned. “But I didn’t click it.”

Nisha peeked at the photograph that struck terror and disgust in her mom’s heart but evoked praise from her dad. “This is mine!” She snatched the photograph.

Now she can show it to her friends, who wouldn’t believe she sees a snake every afternoon. Her special neighbour.

DUCK FOR YOUR DREAMS

Life was full of obstacles for Shyam. Some to be jumped over like hurdles, others to be ducked down or aside.

In the early morning, he had to jump over the gutter and its overflowing contents as he made his way to the toilet shared between ten families. Then back again before his mother shepherded him and his sister out of the locality. The next hurdle was the watchman's baton, which would unerringly block their way as the trio entered the apartment complex where his mother worked as a maid. Although the wooden rod would let his mother pass, it would playfully wave in front of him and his sister, forcing them to jump over. Unavoidable morning exercises.

Then came the problems one had to duck like the shoes flying into his scrawny body, with a yell to be polished until it shone. His mother would flinch every time the boots hit him but not utter a word, thinking of the school fees paid by the arms that flung the offending footwear. His sister, assisting their mother, would dodge the condescending stares of the kids at the breakfast table.

At school, Shyam would often duck the dusters and books flying at his torso, diverting his attention for a split second from the cricket ground outside his window.

Back from school at the same house where he had polished the shoes in the morning, he would duck as the lady of the house would reach out to wring his ears. She knew his mother did not understand the teacher's remarks in his school diary and tried to instil discipline.

One of the biggest hindrances to his happiness was the dining table laden with food. So, he would bend over his notebook, gulping down hungry desires, his head nearly touching that of his sister, who was similarly stooped over by life's burdens. And then he would duck again as life threw snickering remarks at him through laughing eyes and whispered giggles. He was ready to jump, duck, and bend as deemed fit by the world, but only on one condition. The freedom to climb over a wall in the evening.

The wall represented happiness. As soon as Shyam's mother nodded, he headed over to the parapet of the adjacent flat. Climbing over the wall led him straight to the quaint old quarters of Coach Pinto. He shuffled across the veranda and huddled by the window to catch a full view of the television screen at the opposite end of the room. Coach Pinto smiled and inserted a video cassette into his VCR. The chants across the stadium dissolved Shyam's sordid memories of the day. Coach Pinto settled into his armchair with a notebook in his hand and made notes for his students playing on the cricket ground.

While Shyam gobbled the biscuits handed to him, dreaming of someday making it onto the television screen with a bat. He would be the hardest hitter, instilling fear in his opponents, the bowlers. Then, he wouldn't need to duck for his dreams.

THE ROOFTOP ADVENTURE

The afternoon sun was ready to fry an egg. Damu looked as if he would gobble one if he could. The heady smells from the kitchen below made his stomach grumble.

"Are you sure you want to do this now?" He asked Lila as he propped her on the rusty, nearly vertical ladder. Her ten-year-old frail frame belied the hidden reserves of strength she used to swing herself up the rungs.

"Yes. Do you want the juiciest mangoes or not?"

Poor Damu was caught between the culinary wonders happening two stories below and the natural miracles hanging at arm's length from the rooftop. He chose the latter and followed Lila obediently. She was four years younger than Damu, the youngest in the household, but commanded respect with an innate wisdom.

Damu glanced at the brown bag swinging dangerously close to his face. One smack from the bag, and he would find himself lying on the cement floor of the terrace with a broken bone or two. "But why do you have this knapsack?"

"What if we pluck more than we can eat?" Lila answered without turning, her sharp eyes focused on the rungs above.

"Won't uncle scold?"

"He'd be happy to know I am enjoying my summer vacations," Lila chuckled.

Once they hurled themselves onto the rather slippery roof, Damu reached out eagerly to pluck the mangoes.

Lila ignored his efforts and made herself comfortable against the rising pillar of the chimney. It was the only shaded spot. Above her, the mango tree swayed under Damu's ravenous attempts. She took out her book and started reading.

"Lila! Give your knapsack!" Damu was finding it hard to keep the mangoes from rolling along the slope. They tumbled their way to the roof's edge, where the cement ledge stopped them from a further fall. He reached out to pick the mangoes from the rim. A slip of the leg here and the loss of balance there would send him flying below to his grandmother's vegetable garden. The pumpkins could soften the fall. The smell of fried cutlets and fritters made him giddy. He went to the top near the chimney, noting that Lila was unaware of anything that transpired between him and the mangoes.

"So, this is what you had in the knapsack?" he said, looking at the books beside her. He held one up in disdain. "Another mystery? Don't you get bored?"

Lila remained silent.

"Listen, I am going down. Can I borrow your bag?"

Lila flung her empty bag towards him.

"Wonder why they are making cutlets and fritters today," he observed as he packed the mangoes.

Lila looked up from her book. "Guests arriving in the evening. Why do you think I climbed up here?"

Damu stared at her books and then at her. He had a hearty laugh. "So, what do I say if someone asks?" He had a twinkle in his eye.

"That she is off on an adventure," Lila whispered with a conspiratorial nod and a giggle.

YOUNG DREAMS

"Far away there in the sunshine are my highest aspirations. I may not reach them, but I can look up and see their beauty, believe in them, and try to follow where they lead."

– Louisa May Alcott

TO EACH THEIR OWN

Manav's eyes met hers briefly when she entered the coach. He yearned to look at those dark brown eyes again, but a brouhaha interrupted him.

"Whose suitcase is this?" yelled the man who had followed the brown-eyed girl.

A middle-aged woman in a deep red saree jostled the man and peered underneath the seat. She was followed by a squiggly young boy, who disappeared under the berth as he inspected. Four pairs of eyes looked accusingly at Manav's mother sitting in a state of nirvana by the window. "This seat belongs to us," said the woman in red to Manav's mother, who stared back but did not budge.

A flush of embarrassment crept along Manav's neck as he glanced at the doe-eyed girl. She stared back in disdain. His father, to his right, kept punctuating the air with strange gestures in a brave attempt to lure his wife to his side of the compartment.

"Ma!" Manav called out in anger and shame. He nudged the scrawny little girl sitting to his left. She shuffled towards the window to allow her mother to sit beside her.

Manav held up his hand to seek a truce with the other family. He knew his mother would have surreptitiously pushed the errant suitcase underneath the opposite berth. Manav pulled it out amid loud protests from his mother.

When he was a teen, his mother would pull out offending magazines from his bedcovers. Now, it was his turn to take the moral high ground. Goaded by his angry looks, she heaved up and plonked herself next to him.

The new family and their luggage now had space, and the friction was mitigated. However, the air that was warm with anticipation when the new family entered the compartment had now turned cold. There was utter silence as the families sized each other up - two fathers, two mothers, a son and daughter, a daughter and son. What a perfect match, thought Manav as he stole glances at the doe-eyed girl. The introduction could have been better.

The boy memorized the girl's appearance while the family negotiated and reconciled with the cramped space between them.

She wore a yellow tunic over a pair of denim leggings. Her brown hair was tied into a loose ponytail. The tip of her nose pointed slightly towards the ceiling as if she couldn't tolerate the stench emanating from the train floor. Her face turned away from both the families, glowed intermittently under the passing station lights. Her hand lay protectively over a handbag on her lap while silver earrings dangled from her delicate ears in sync with the train's rhythm. Overall, it was an appearance that pleased him.

"I am hungry!" the girl's younger brother proclaimed to no one. The lady in red grunted.

"Ma, I want some chips," Manav's sister whispered into her mother's ears. The mother handed her a packet of chips and smirked at the mother of the opposite faction, who had not yet heeded her son's hungry call.

"Can I go up to the top berth?" Manav's sister added another request.

"Of course, of course. Munna, can you help Mona climb up to the top?"

Manav winced. His mother insisted on calling him Munna, which sounded like the name of a ten-year-old or a hustler, neither of which was a flattering representation of a young man in his teens wanting to impress a girl. He hazarded a glance at the girl in the yellow tunic. Did she have a sneer on her lips? As he helped Mona, the girl's mother delivered a sermon to her son on good eating habits.

"Rohit, you know it's too close to your dinner time, so you can't have snacks. And do you remember what I told you about snacks on the train? They are not good for you. I have packed homemade snacks. We have the entire day tomorrow. You can enjoy them."

Evidently, the sermon on snacks was meant for Manav's mother. He let out an inaudible sigh. Why do women always start out like this when they meet? They compare, contrast, condescend, and close their minds. He wished the mothers had been long-lost friends. Then they would have been happy to meet each other again. They would have discussed their families. "Oh, you have a daughter and son? I have a son and a daughter!" His mother would have exclaimed at the obvious. Subsequently, the two estranged friends would have exchanged meaningful glances. During the thirty-six-hour journey, there would be snatched conversations, stolen glimpses, perhaps a touch here, a graze there. By the end of the trip, the entire family would have been friends with each other. Invitations might have been extended for home visits, and he would have the opportunity to look at those doe eyes again...

The train jolted Manav out of his daydreams. The girl in the yellow kurta was missing. The mother dozed and swayed to the rhythm of the train. The father looked awkwardly into the middle distance while his parents teetered and leaned onto each other as they napped.

Manav stood as if to stretch and balanced himself by holding the top berth. The girl's brother sat on the top with a comic book in his lap and a handful of potato chips spread on the open page. Manav's gaze lingered on the potato chips.

"I didn't take them. She gave them to me!" The boy defended, pointing at Mona.

"He looked hungry, Bhaiyya!" Mona explained plaintively.

Manav smiled at the boy. Should he ask him about his sister? He glanced at Rohit's father sitting below and immediately knew that although his gaze was stuck somewhere ahead, his ears were clued to any conversation upstairs.

Manav made his way slowly toward the toilets. He held his breath as he reached the end of the coach. It was not the stench that made him do it but the vision of yellow moving toward him. As she waited for him to make way and let her pass, he released his breath, and a whiff of fragrance hit his nostrils.

The girl made her way back to her seat. Manav turned around to follow her but caught a grin on the face of the man sitting straight across. He grabbed the berth exaggeratedly and resumed his swagger towards the toilet, cursing the grinning man under his breath. When he returned, the girl was sitting comfortably by the window. Manav sat by the opposite window and closed his eyes.

The fragrance added a mystique to his daydream. The train slowed down and came to a halt. Outside, it was abuzz with activity. Passengers spilled out with their luggage, and some just hopped for a stroll. Others ran to the stalls to buy refreshments, food, and anything to read. A man dressed in a railway uniform stopped by their compartment with a red-coloured box at his hip. He quickly scanned the two families and confirmed their preferences.

"Meals? Non-vegetarian meals?"

"Yes," the two fathers replied in unison. Smiles appeared to thaw the ice at last.

As the pantry staff moved on, the girl's father handed out the parcels to the entire group. The families ate in silence, but something changed between them. The shared dinner preferences highlighted a commonality amidst the invisible rife.

"I wish we had brought some bananas with us," said Manav's father to no one in particular, but the girl's father pricked up his ears.

"We have some with us. Don't we?" the girl's father turned to his wife as he asked.

"Yes, yes," the girl's mother beamed while Manav's mother shuffled uncomfortably in her seat.

The sharing of the bananas opened up a channel for communication.

"We usually carry fruits with us when we travel," the girl's father said amicably to Manav's father.

"Are you travelling back to Bombay?" Manav's father asked.

"Yes, the vacation is over, sadly. Now we have to wait until next year. These bananas are from my father's orchard."

"They are delicious. How long have you lived in Bombay?"

"Nearly twenty years," the girl's father replied.

"We'll complete twenty-six this year," Manav's father shared.

Manav listened to this conversation half-heartedly. These were the usual ice-breakers whenever they met a new family on the train. They travelled on this route twice a year, and the introduction always started with the 'how many years in Bombay' question.

The foundation for all further communication between the passengers would be the number of years spent in the city. If one of the families was a newbie, the conversation would veer towards finding accommodation, the best suburbs to live in, good schools, places to hang out, and sometimes, the exchange of references in the search for a job.

If the families were even-keeled in terms of their residence in the city, the exchange would be more about the vagaries of city life. There would be an exchange of anecdotes about the fast-paced city with a large heart, a comparison of life in the city and elsewhere, and a cautious benchmarking of each other's progress on the city's social ladder.

"Do you own an apartment? In the suburbs? East or West? 1 BHK or a 2 BHK? How far is your place from the station? Such questions would follow, allowing the families to measure up against each other and classify into categories - lower middle class, middle class, upper-middle-class, but invariably the middle class.

Manav observed how predictable these conversations were while nodding politely. Despite these banters and heart-to-heart conversations, the connection rarely progressed beyond the train carriage. As soon as they disembarked, the families forgot each other.

Manav was hoping that it would be different this time. Occasionally, he glanced at the girl who was reading. Happy at discovering a hobby he shared with the girl, he turned to the men and realised in horror that he was the topic of his father's monologue. His lacklustre education and lack of ambition were presented at length. The girl's mother tut-tutted regularly, and his mother soaked up the sympathy. The girl's father looked at Manav, sometimes with scorn and other times with disinterest.

"Manav says he wants to be a writer! Tell me, sir, do you think it will do him any good?" his father complained.

Prickly embarrassment stirred behind Manav's neck for the second time since meeting the girl. He glanced at her, but she appeared oblivious to the discussion and was engrossed in her book.

"Thank God for small mercies. Our daughter wants to become a doctor," the girl's mother beamed. "Or an engineer," continued her father, "depending on whether she scores higher in Biology or Mathematics."

"Impressive!" Manav's father retorted and glanced at Manav, who could hear the unspoken words, 'Did you hear that? Engineer or a Doctor!'

"He took up Arts after his tenth grade," Manav's father said in a low voice as if apologising for his son's choice.

"I have enrolled at St. Xavier's College. It is one of the best colleges in India." Manav's ego had stirred up.

"But what good will it do for your career?" The girl's father crossed his arms across his chest and waited for Manav to answer.

"We have good placements, sir, err, uncle."

The man smirked and let out an involuntary chuckle. "I think it's time to sleep," he suggested, consoling Manav's father with a nod.

The families shuffled around as they prepared their respective berths to sleep. The younger children slept along with their mothers in the lowermost berths. The fathers climbed onto the middle berths while Manav and the girl climbed onto the top berths.

Manav stared at the ceiling for a while, then stretched his hand to pick up the water bottle from the holder between the berths. While doing so, his eyes scanned the opposite berth. The girl was writing in a diary. She must have felt his stare because she closed the notebook and looked directly at him. She was not angry, nor did she smile. She merely looked through him, unsettling him. He took one of his books from his bag and pretended to read. The girl looked at the paperback with some interest. Manav's lips curled up into a smile. He had caught her attention.

"What book is that?" she asked. Her voice was as steady as her gaze. Pleasant to hear, Manav thought.

"It's a John Grisham novel," Manav said without turning his head.

"Can I borrow it tomorrow?"

"Of course!"

The girl then proceeded to write. But the brief interaction emboldened Manav.

"Do you like John Grisham's books?"

"Huh?

"Do you like... Have you read his books before?"

"I have read one book - The Rainmaker."

"Nice. Did you like it? They have made it into a movie. Though I don't think it'll be released in India."

"It was ok. I read during my last term break. It's the only book I have read in the last two years."

"Why so?"

"I was busy preparing for my boards."

"Aah, yes, the boards!" The mention of examinations silenced the youth for a while.

"So, how did they go?"

"The exams? They were fine."

"So, a doctor, eh?"

The girl shrugged.

"I am in my second year of BA," Manav continued.

"Ok."

After this, Manav was at a loss for words. Should I ask her name? He sat brooding over this question for a while. Finally, he drew up his breath and turned to the girl, only to find her fast asleep. Manav turned off his reading light.

When he woke up the next day, his eyes instinctively moved to his left. The berth was empty. He leaned over to the edge of the berth to look at the occupants of the seats below. His fondness for sleep had made him miss the further thawing of differences between the two families.

The fathers sat side by side, engrossed in discussions. The girl's father spoke as if dispensing pertinent stock market advice, and his father listened like an eager but naive investor. The mothers were not visible, and he guessed they might be engaged in a similar heart-to-heart conversation right below his berth. But the sight that warmed the cockles of his heart and captured his imagination was the girl playing with the two children. Her laughter was as cheerful as the rising sun, and her smile as fresh as the morning dew. She giggled when Mona said something and warned Rohit when he tried to snatch a piece of apple from Mona.

Apple! The sight of the apple reminded him of breakfast. He looked at his watch. It was nearly 11 am. He hoped there was something to eat because the next long halt for the train might only be for lunch. As he climbed down from his berth, he heard sniggers from the two women.

"You missed your breakfast," said his mother. He nodded and walked off towards the toilets. When he returned, a sandwich packet waited for him on his seat. He stepped gingerly over the sandals and shoes strewn on the floor and reached for the pack.

"Say thanks to Sinha Aunty here," his mother poked him in his ribs. How he wished she would stop doing it.

"Thanks, Aunty," though he wasn't sure why he thanked her. He was famished, and if he had to thank someone before eating the sandwich, so be it. As he munched hungrily, he felt a tingling on his face. He stopped and looked at her. Her eyes were on him briefly but turned away as soon as he looked up. That's some progress, he thought and smiled.

"Manav, did you hear what Uncle said?" Manav's father looked at him expectantly. He had definitely not, but he looked at Sinha Uncle to express his interest.

"You should pursue an MBA after graduation. It doesn't matter which course you choose for your undergraduate studies. Getting a business degree will bring you to par with the more intelligent students," Mr. Sinha leaned forward as he spoke. His face reflected the satisfaction of dispensing the right directions to a lost soul.

Manav cleared his throat and looked at his father. He looked at the girl. She was listening attentively. "But uncle, I have several intelligent friends who don't have a business degree and are doing extremely well in life."

Mr. Sinha leaned back and looked at Manav's father with a smirk.

Manav's father looked apologetic. "I have been telling him, sir. He doesn't even need to do an MBA. He just needs to learn the basics of computers and stick with me. He can run the shop for me."

"You have a shop?"

"Yes, sir. I own an electronic goods shop. I plan to expand to computers and set up an internet cafe." Manav's father lowered his voice. "I hear it will be a very profitable business, but I need someone to help me with computers. I was hoping that he would," he nodded towards Manav.

"But, Daddy, if I was interested in computers, I would have taken up science after tenth grade."

Manav's father slumped further into his seat.

Mr. Sinha now looked in pity at both father and son. "Look at my daughter Riya here. It would be best if she gets a seat in a medical college. If not, she can take up computer engineering and maybe later get a business degree."

Manav glanced at Riya, who seemed to be lost in her thoughts. Her face was turned towards the window.

"Engineering and then an MBA?" Manav's father asked Mr. Sinha.

"Yes, I have met so many successful people in my company. I am a science graduate who ended up in a clerical job at a huge organization. I had to work hard to earn the three promotions I received. By the time I retire, I might get one more. But do you know something? Fresh MBA graduates join at the level that I am right now."

Manav's father let out a gasp and looked incredulously at him.

Mr. Sinha looked at Manav, who remained unimpressed.

"To each his own," Mr. Sinha shrugged as he said.

There was silence as the three men contemplated their respective concerns. Manav was happy that he now knew her name - Riya. Manav's father wondered if he had made a mistake by setting up a business. Mr. Sinha prayed that his daughter would get into one of the professions.

The two women who had been listening to the men so far shared apprehensions about their children. Surprisingly, their voices had dropped to whispers. Manav had butterflies in his stomach as they kept looking at him and Riya intermittently. What if?

As the day passed, their parents continued their banter while the younger ones played with each other. Riya picked up her book again, leaving Manav with no choice but to close his eyes and nap.

By evening, both families had grown tired of the train journey and each other. The parents had split. The children fought over one of the comic books. Manav and Riya sat in their own morose corners. It had grown dark, and the landscape outside offered no succour. The dinner was eaten quietly, and no food was shared.

The next day, as the train pulled into their destination, Manav's father wrangled a smile out of his tired face and pulled out a visiting card.

"Mr. Sinha, please visit us whenever you plan to buy a computer for your daughter. We'll have everything ready in six months."

Mr. Sinha nodded pleasantly and proceeded to collect their belongings. He knew he could get a better deal from his company but didn't share it aloud.

The two families disembarked at the station and waved statutory goodbyes. Manav waited for a few seconds and continued to stare at Riya. She never looked back. He sighed and turned around, but not before seeing Mr. Sinha throw his father's visiting card onto the train tracks.

Manav's throat choked up. To each their own, he surmised. And she didn't even return the John Grisham book!

LILA'S PLAN

Lila had a plan. She focused her gaze at a distance. For the first time in her life, she felt brave and important. She had to take matters into her hands.

The plan gained urgency with each passing day. Every day, she wished she had done something different. Something other than cowering and hiding.

She had to push back. She had to stand up for what she believed. Tomorrow, she would act according to her plan. It will be all action and no passive acceptance.

Lila woke up early the next day and packed her things. The bag was heavy, plus she had to sling two more tools on her shoulder. The load was familiar. Lila carried it daily, but it had a specific purpose today. The heaviness did not bother her as much as the volume. To carry out her plan, she had to be stealthy. You can't take up too much space when you want to exercise your freedom against society's misgivings. You start small and then expand until you claim your space one day.

Lila reached the station at the planned time. The digital display at the station showed 8:15 a.m. She scanned the perimeter. Everything looked okay. Everyone was busy. No stares, lecherous grins, or offensive lyrics sung in equally repulsive tones. She adjusted her dupatta to bring the loose ends to the front. It was a critical manoeuvre. She couldn't be yanked back by the crowd while boarding. That would be fatal.

The train was approaching. Lila could see the passengers moving to strategic positions in tandem.

Lila swung her bag to the front in one swift motion. The tools will have to stay on her right shoulder. She felt calmer. The burlesque bag protected her from frontal assault while the tools blocked overtures from behind.

She had to secure her diminishing perimeter.

The train lunged forward, its contents spilling onto the platform. The crowd surged forward like breeding fishes leaping cross-current, not knowing if they would survive.

Lila steadied her breath. The crowd carried her ahead in a single wave-like motion. Her instincts made her lift her foot onto the train just in time. There was no way she could see where her legs would go. Her left hand grabbed the steel rod in the middle. It shone like a divine lifeline.

That's it! She was in. Soon, Lila will have to tackle her nemesis. But now was the time to wait and catch her breath.

The train lurched into the next station in precisely three minutes, and the action began!

The crowd nearly swept Lila off her feet, but she tightened the grip on the overhead bars. They cursed her big bag and her spiky tools. She closed her eyes and let it all pass. A narrow space cleared for a few seconds, and she moved to the side in a single diagonal push. Reaching the compartment partition, she spied her nemesis through the door. Lila pushed through the crowd with all her might. Her nemesis eyed the space right next to the door. Lila jostled until she found a nook. Her rival, dressed in a blue saree, smirked.

"You again?" her scheming eyes asked.

"Yes!" Lila's eyes replied.

The lady snuggled into her corner by the door.

Lila positioned her tools— the roll pack and her drafter— one on either shoulder. She took her book from the bag and then placed the bag between her feet on the floor.

"So, a book again, huh?" This time, the lady spoke out aloud.

Lila smiled in reply.

"And all this trouble in a crowded train to find a spot to read?"

Lila did not acknowledge the remark.

"I don't understand how you engineering students can afford to read such trash." The lady uttered with a sickly-sweet smile.

Lila nodded. "I am reading aloud. Do you mind?"

The smile disappeared. "No, wait!"

But Lila was off to Blanding's Castle. Before they reached the next station, she heard chuckles from beside her.

Lila's plan had worked in all its Wodehousian glory.

THE NEW JOB

The job, the apartment, her technicoloured dreams had come true.

Eka squinted at the vehicles plying below. If she narrowed her eyes enough, she could imagine them as ants with lights on them. That is an idea she could use. Ants with lights.

She turned her gaze to the apartment. Garish and loud are the adjectives that fit the homeowner. The apartment carried his essence. She will have to redo the paint and the upholstery, but she was always up for a design challenge.

A knock on the door. Eka nearly sang out aloud. The men came in with their hullaballoos. "Your address is hard to find. We had to wait more than an hour before we could use the lift. The stuff is heavy. We haven't had lunch."

Eka dished out a couple of notes and sent them out the door. She unpacked the items and stared at them lovingly. Her phone rang.

"Eka, have you reached safely?"

"Yes, Ma."

"Is it a good apartment?"

"It's gorgeous."

"Now, listen carefully. Papa is furious."

"Why?"

"Who is this Bobby, and why is he calling up, asking for you?"

Eka sat up excitedly. "Oh! Bobby called? I'll return his call, don't worry."

"But who is he? And what is this place he was talking about? Have you rented a place along with him?"

"Ma, don't worry. I will explain everything at the right time."

"But we don't understand. First, you said you wanted to learn the arts, then interior design, then you kept drawing pictures of tables and chairs, and now you have joined a graphic design company. And there's a Bobby?"

"Relax, Ma," Eka crooned as she settled in her favourite chair.

"The graphic design company pays well. Bobby is my manager."

"Are you reporting to him? He sounded a bit rough. And what about the place?"

"He reports to me, Ma. He'll be my factory manager. And the place is not far from our home."

Eka ran her fingers over the smooth surface of the armchair. "You remember the pictures of the tables and chairs, Ma? You will see them all come to life soon."

Eka beamed at her furniture. They winked back at her.

THE PROMOTION

The storm that began at five in the morning continued unabated until eight. Not the kind where the wind shrieks and the rain drenches in buckets but the kind where buckets get their handles yanked off, the utensils suffer falls, and the family goes about in silence.

The lady of the house was angry. Her woman Friday was not in for work yet.

If it was not for the 8:23 local train that she caught without fail every morning, the family members would have received an earful. But neither the train nor the family would wait for her rants. So, instead, she expressed her anger at the inanimate objects in the house.

The next morning, the storm grew louder. For the second day in a row, the lady of the house scampered around, completing her morning routine.

"I am sure she has gone off for some wedding in the family. She could have told me, right?" the lady yelled at the dog that cowered in the corner. Others shuffled out of the way like the passengers at the railway station when a fast train whistles past.

A week passed by without any trace of the absconding help. The lady now fretted and fumed every minute.

"Should I employ someone else?" she asked the man who pretended to read the newspaper.

"Will you help me in the morning?" she asked the teen, who pretended to sleep.

"Can you adjust with bread and jam?" she asked the child, who pretended to sulk.

"Do you want to go for a walk?" she asked the dog, who did not pretend but wagged his tail.

She set out with the dog on a leash. "How I wish I had my life on a leash!" she thought.

To her pleasant surprise, a familiar face loomed on the horizon. The prodigal maid had returned.

The lady ushered her in with great fanfare. A special poha and piping hot tea appeared magically from the kitchen. The helper grinned as she handed a packet. "An offering from our temple. I prayed for you. Did you get your promotion?"

The lady beamed ear to ear. "I did! And now I need you even more. So never leave without warning again."

The woman Friday nodded in all solemnity. "What would you do without me?"

"Indeed!"

The lady went to sleep dreaming of the 8:23 local in peace.

PURPOSE

"There is nothing in the world, I venture to say that would so effectively help one survive even the worst conditions as the knowledge that there is a meaning in one's life."

– Viktor Frankl

UPSTREAM

The empty street picked up all the noises from the neighbourhood. The wailing baby in the yellow house, the loud TV in the blue house, the noisy jackdaws on the mango trees in front of the eerily quiet bungalow, the constantly yelling couples in the posh European-style villa, and the giggling child in front of the red-roofed double-storied house.

Mithun strode through the street as if he was passing through in a hurry. But he observed every little detail.

Mithun walked daily for a week, wearing a heat-resistant T-shirt, cargo pants, and matching athletic shoes. He would ride his bicycle to the post office in the adjoining lane, park it by the lamppost, and walk straight into the street.

At the end of the street, Mithun would turn left into a narrow path that led to the river. He would spend ten minutes gazing into the water, then walk straight back, avoiding the street he came through. Instead, he would turn ninety degrees onto another road that returned to the post office.

Anyone following him would think this man was merely walking to the river and back.

Mithun, on the other hand, was onto a plan. He observed minute details of the street during his daily walk and nightly run. Tall deciduous trees lined the road on both sides, and several streetlights blinked precariously. All the families owned two cars or more. Most of the houses remained quiet during the day. The occupants were out working or studying, except for the wailing baby and its nanny.

Mithun had zeroed in on two targets for his day job. The blue-walled house with the loud TV was perfect with a low compound wall, an old couple living alone, and no visible helpers around. The TV would drown out any possible sounds while breaking in.

The red-roofed house was the second. It was covered with trees, making it difficult for walkers to discern any movement in the compound. And it was at the end of the street, perfect for a getaway. However, the giggling child in the front yard was a deterrent. Mithun had seen her playing in front of the house four of the seven days he walked by. It was difficult to predict her presence.

An old woman stared out a window on the first floor. She did not seem to notice him. He tested her presence of mind by moving near the wall and waving to her. She did not budge, and neither did she move her gaze.

But the child saw him and waved back with a giggle.

Mithun was uncertain about this one, but the blue-walled house was a sitting duck for a daytime project.

Day jobs were more complicated than night jobs, but Mithun preferred working in broad daylight. It gave him a sense of respectability. His ambition had been to be a sports coach someday. He was pretty athletic at school. But family circumstances forced him to drop out and look for odd jobs.

Turning towards crime was easy as he strayed further from his chosen path. He found a Guru, became his student, then his assistant, and then branched out independently. His athletic abilities became handy.

When Mithun met his old games teacher a year later, he couldn't look him in the eye. By then, there were rumours about his involvement in a few petty cases in the neighbourhood.

"Do you remember how you used to love swimming upstream, Mithun?" his teacher asked.

Mithun's eyes lit up. "Yes, I loved the challenge!"

"Why are you drifting downstream in life then?"

Mithun hung his head and walked away. It was easy for others to say. Would they offer him a respectable job instead?

The conversation did nothing to change his means of livelihood, but it changed the way he dressed, talked, and walked. Now, he emulated the respectable members of the society. He wore only expensive clothes and accessories, doing double shifts to support his classy lifestyle.

Mithun developed a modus operandi. He knew that the affluent often stepped out for exercise in residential areas. Mithun imitated these rich, health-conscious folks and went for daily brisk walks or jogs. He was always casually but impeccably dressed on such outings. After he did a recce of a neighbourhood, he would choose a target for a day job or a night job.

This particular street near the river was his latest work site. Mithun walked hurriedly down the street on a bright, sunny afternoon. The servants would have retired for a nap in the quiet, invisible corners of the houses.

The blue-walled house was set away from the road, and the driveway curved inside. Mithun paused at the gate, glanced around, and swiftly hid behind a tree near the wall. He grabbed the wall with both hands and hauled himself halfway up before freezing mid-jump.

A dog lay a few metres away from the wall, in the porch's shade. Damn! How had he not noticed this creature before? He lowered himself onto the ground slowly and leaned against the wall. His heart thumped wildly. It was a close call. The wily beast did not bark at him but glared intently.

Mithun was sure that even if he wasn't caught, he would be at the doctor's clinic suffering an injection for a dog bite. His eyes strayed across the street to the red-roofed house.

Should he take a chance?

The disappointment of finding a dog at his target house whipped him into a frenzy, and he took the leap. Standing outside the compound wall of the red-roofed house, he was surprised to find the child missing from the front yard.

Perfect!

The compound wall was higher than the first one, but he clambered over with practised dexterity. He gulped as he saw the old woman sitting by the window. She showed no sign of recognition or fright.

Was she blind?

Mithun crept forward stealthily. All his senses were focused on the mission ahead. An open door, window, or back door was all he needed. He had his tools tucked in safely inside his cargo pants.

Mithun smiled as he spied an open window near the porch. But with his next step, two things happened. He stepped on a pile of crunchy dry leaves, and the iron bars of the window above started ringing frantically.

Mithun stepped back in fright and moved further from the house for a better view of the window upstairs. The old woman was banging on the iron bars with a steel plate. To make things worse, she started wailing loudly.

What ruckus!

Mithun did not wait for another second and ran around the house to reach the river at the back. He had planned his escape route. But just as he skipped down the concrete steps to the river, he heard a scream, and a second wailing voice joined that of the old woman.

Confused, Mithun crouched behind a boulder, and that's when he saw her. A white frock bobbing up and down in the water. He raced to the bank and jumped right in. She was not led adrift far by the current, and he could reach her quickly. Hauling up to the bank, he heard the wailing voice come nearer.

A woman in a nightie came running down the steps, calling, "Baby! Poor Baby! God save her!"

He laid the child on the bank and pressed her tummy to let the water out. She coughed, spluttered, and opened her eyes briefly to give him the most beautiful smile he had ever seen.

The child was breathing and alive. The woman gathered her up in her arms and thanked him profusely. She tried hard to join her hands in gratitude, but the child's weight bore down on her arms.

"Thank you, Sir! Thank you very much, Sir!" her eyes reflected nothing but respect.

Mithun joined his hands and asked her to immediately get the child to a doctor.

The woman clambered up the steps, thanking the almighty.

Mithun shook himself and wiped away the water from his face. As he turned towards the river, he heard an unmistakable giggle. The same laugh Mithun had heard innumerable times before while recceing the street. The same child who would wave back at him and whom he saved from the river today.

Mithun sat down by the riverbank. After many years, he did something that earned him respect. Mithun threw a twig into the river and saw it swiftly descend with the current. He then stood up with a determined push, pulled out all his tools, and threw them into the water.

His eyes wandered further up the river, where on a hillock was the police training institute. He will have to start with his school exams, but what is life without a challenge? Close by, a tiny boat bobbed lazily in the water. Mithun untied the boat, grabbed the oars, and frantically rowed upstream.

THE SHED

The sawing and planing of wood happened non-stop at Mani's workshop. He closed his eyes, sitting in an armchair he designed for his father. It had withstood the vagaries of time and now offered him a few blissful minutes in the afternoon.

His wife often wondered how he could nap in the background of all the carpentry work inside his shop, but to Mani, those sounds were like lullabies. He had grown up amidst the chopping, clanging, and thumping, learned the craft from his father, started a business, and succeeded enough to afford a modest two-storied house and a motorcycle. His father would have been proud.

Mani felt proud of himself, too, of his achievements. But his mind was not at peace. Try as he might, he couldn't go to sleep. He had handed over his business to his oldest apprentice. The accounts were handled by his wife. His children were studying in one of the best schools in the town and doing well. So, what was he worried about?

By next year, he would save enough to exchange the motorcycle for a car. He had five more years until his eldest daughter chose a university course. Enough time to build a corpus. No, it wasn't money or the lack of it that bothered him. It was something else.

Mani would lay awake at night, imagining his father working in the shack attached to their kitchen. The shed stood empty. Mani's business outgrew his father's petty ambitions and the shed. He was successful, yet happiness eluded him.

Thunder clapped, and Mani rushed out of bed to check if the workshop windows were shut tight. Earlier in the evening, the sky had sulked. The night allowed the sky to open the floodgates. He did not go back to bed; instead, he slept in the armchair, guarding the workshop. When the rain stopped, the sun arrived, ignorant of the night's stormy shenanigans. The birds began chirping, and the sounds of dawn woke him up.

Mani yawned and pushed himself out of the armchair. His workmen trooped in for the day while he strolled for cursory supervision. That's when he heard the boy.

Hidden behind a workbench, the boy hummed a sordid tune. Only when he wiped his face did Mani realize he was crying. "Why is he crying?" Mani asked the boy's father, his employee.

"The water came inside our house yesterday."

"Is this the first time?"

"No, but it's the first time he lost his books. We were saving the hens and forgot about his books lying on the floor."

Mani turned to the boy. "Why did you leave your books on the floor?" "That's where I always keep them," he replied between sobs.

"Don't tell me you don't have a safer place!"

The boy looked at Mani in surprise. "No, we don't."

Later in the evening, an idea took shape as Mani watched the boy leave with his father.

A glimmer of hope shone through the dusk. Mani slept soundly and woke up at dawn with renewed vigour. In his father's abandoned shack, he began his personal project. A high shelf and table for the boy who lost his books to the flooded floor.

THE TANGENTIAL

Mathew jogged the last hundred metres, bringing his breath under control and relinquishing the obsession with his limbs. They were now free to choose their pace. He could feel the cellular protests tingling all over his leg muscles. Ten rounds of the park, which was nearly ten kilometres.

An excellent running day. But that did not solve Mathew's problem. He was chewing on a particularly tricky situation at work. He had hoped that the exercise would stimulate his brain as well. It didn't.

"Hey, Mathew!" A familiar voice hollered from behind him. It was Silvy, a quick but temperamental runner.

"Aah! How many?" Mathew stammered, his voice rasping in a flurry of breaths.

Silvy held up seven fingers. Mathew nodded. Yes! He had done it again. His run was longer than Silvy's.

"Seven in?" Mathew continued as he walked towards the cafe at the park entrance.

"Ninety."

"Beat you again!" Mathew flashed a smile of satisfaction. "I ran ten in hundred, Ha!"

Silvy waved his hand as he sat down at an empty table. Mathew joined him.

"I thought you'd be happy." Silvy nodded at the cafe employee as he spoke to Mathew. It was a sign to bring them their regulars.

"I am," Mathew replied without looking up his phone.

"Hard to believe."

"Why?" Mathew was still scrolling through his phone.

"Your eyes, your face, tell a different story, man!" Silvy said with a chuckle.

Mathew looked up in surprise.

"You look harassed, to be honest," Silvy continued.

"Not harassed, Silvy, just tired, bored, perhaps."

"Bored? Of running?"

"And other things."

Silvy leaned forward. "I am listening."

"Well, I am stuck with a problem at work. It's not new. We have solved it before. But it keeps recurring in different ways. The cause is different every time, but the effect remains the same."

"Isn't that why you run every day?" Silvy asked with a grin.

Mathew got the drift. He once told Silvy that health was not the only reason he ran. Running helped him think and be creative about his problems.

"But this time, running is not helping." Mathew shook his head. "And look at this track. No change in the last three years. It is the same thing over and over again. I feel like I am going in circles on the track and in life. No progress."

Silvy laughed out loud.

"This is no laughing matter."

"Indeed," Silvy straightened his face and back. "Let me show you something." He took out his phone, swiped a few times, and held it up for Mathew to see.

Mathew gazed at the screen out of politeness and then gasped in astonishment. "Impossible!"

Silvy laughed again.

"But you ran only seven rounds? How can the app show more than ten kilometres?"

Their drinks arrived, and Silvy took his time to enjoy his first few sips.

"Matt, have you noticed a path leading away from the track soon after the five hundred metres mark?"

"No."

"Well, there is such a path. It goes off on a tangential from the running track. You can't miss it. It is right next to the toilets."

"Aah! Now I remember. But isn't that a dirt track going uphill?"

"Yes," Silvy replied with a mischievous smile. "Few people care to run up there, but those who do get to see some of the most beautiful things in the park. I could show you some pictures I took, but I won't spoil your fun. Experience it yourself. And, also get five hundred metres more to each running round." He punctured the morning air with laughter.

Mathew stared at Silvy as if he had shown him a magic trick.

“Try the tangential sometimes, Matt. It might bring some magic into your life.”

LETTING GO

"Some of us think holding on makes us strong; but sometimes it is letting go."

– Herman Hesse

AN EVENING AT THE PARK

Shanti shuffled over to the accounts department's cupboard and placed the file on the topmost shelf, as she did every evening. The usually grumpy Vimala, who sat beside the cupboard, smiled at Shanti. She smiled back. "Looks like someone got a new saree. I have a similar one. I'll wear it tomorrow."

Vimala opened her mouth to say something but remained mute in confusion.

Shanti returned to her desk and called for Pinto, the peon, to get a cup of tea. Pinto appeared almost magically at her elbow with a cup of tea and two biscuits in a saucer.

"What's special today, Pinto?" Shanti asked with a wink.

"Madam, you..." Pinto's voice trailed off as he saw their office manager walk towards Shanti's desk.

"It's already five, Shanti. Aren't you leaving?" the manager asked with a smile and a nod.

Shanti gasped. "Pinto, did you hear that? Just look out of the window. Is the sun setting in the east today?"

Pinto chuckled and shook his head. "You should leave, Madam. This is your chance."

"You are right," Shanti said abruptly. She grabbed her bag, stuffed her lunchbox, found her umbrella under her table, and set off into the evening sun.

A few metres from her office, there was a park. She would often see the elderly enjoying the evening breeze. Today, there was a group of children, too. There was another difference. Shanti saw the park in daylight for the first time in many years. She saw the lush green grass shine. She listened to the birds singing their last songs for the day.

Shanti sat down on the park bench. It did not hurt to enjoy the evening for a few minutes. From where she sat, she could see the office building. Without warning, tears rolled down her eyes. Will she ever get a chance to revisit the park?

Vimala and Pinto arrived in time to see Shanti wipe away her tears. "We will miss you too, Madam. It's time to enjoy your retirement."

WHO WILL REMEMBER ME?

Ashok wrapped his shawl tighter and adjusted his monkey cap. He made a mental note to buy a walking stick. Stepping out before daybreak was becoming more and more difficult. The mornings were colder than last year, and his bones were weaker. Four packets of milk lay in his basket tied at the front gate. One for him and three for Saleema's family.

"Uncle, I'll drop four packets in your basket tomorrow. Would you mind giving it to your neighbours at the back?" the boy asked one day when he came for the money.

"Why can't you give it yourself?"

The boy scratched his head. "The path is rough. It takes me fifteen minutes to reach their house. I often miss my college bus."

Ashok agreed. Couldn't deny a boy his education, could he? So, Ashok carried the three milk packets over the rocky, narrow path along his compound wall every morning, stepping gingerly over gnarly roots, mossy stones, and tiny puddles. He couldn't understand why it took a healthy young boy fifteen minutes to traverse five hundred metres. It took him ten.

The last hurdle on the obstacle course was the wooden picket, which had to be jumped over. Ashokan was tall enough to comfortably clamber over it, but his legs had begun to protest lately. He would place the packets on the porch, seeing no one but hearing wailing children, kitchen utensils, and sometimes, shouting men.

His next errand was to protect Maakan's newspaper from the birds. They were particularly attracted to juicy gossip and breaking news. Ashok would trudge back the path, catch his breath at the stile near his gate, and then proceed to Maakan's house. The newspaper would be lying on the driveway leading to the gate. Ashok would pick it up and place it inside the mailbox to the left of the entrance, facing the house, a place convenient for Maakan but inconvenient for the newspaper boy.

His next stop was at Menon's beautiful villa. It was an object of envy and pride for the neighbourhood— blue and white, serene and spacious. Menon maintained it well but could do little to save his hibiscus flowers hanging lazily across the wall. Morning walkers plucked the flowers, leaving nothing for Menon for his morning pooja. For some strange reason, the flowers bloomed only to the side of the road and not inside his lawn. So, Ashok would pluck a few for his good friend and tuck them inside the milk basket, away from lascivious eyes.

There was an additional errand now. Ashok had to water Lakshmi's plants. She was in the United States with her children, the six-monthly vacation she was accorded in her sixties. Ashok made a mental note to water the plants in the evening.

He rushed home, opened his gate, unlocked his front door, and removed a notepad from his desk drawer. Buy a walking stick. Water Lakshmi's plants. He heaved a sigh of relief.

If he didn't write it down, he was sure to forget. Then, he wondered, do these people remember me? Lakshmi called him a week ago to remind him about the plants, but he hadn't met anyone in person for six months, except for the milk boy who came for his monthly payments. He would disappear, too, as he switched to online payments.

The next day, Ashok trudged down to Saleema's house as usual. He made a mental note again to buy a walking stick. The path had become rougher after the rains washed away the soil among the rocks.

On the way back, he tripped and fell. His knees suffered the weight of his clumsy body. He used his hand to break the fall, so his limb took a hit, too.

Ashok looked around. Not a soul in sight. He picked himself up and hobbled back to his house. He had to rest, but he felt anxious. His errands needed to be completed. The next day, too, he stayed at home.

A lonely old man in a lonely old house, he whispered to himself. Where are the people now? He missed his Radha, his soulmate. They never had children, but both kept themselves busy with their jobs. Retirement hit them hard, especially Radha. She passed away a year after she retired, leaving Ashok to cope with the loneliness and the emptiness.

Was life worth living at all? He tried to keep busy, but for whom? Who will remember me?

Someone rang the bell. It was Saleema. "Ashok Uncle, what happened? I was worried."

Ashok smiled gratefully. People remembered him, after all. He asked Saleema if she could boil some tea. "I have visitors," he said with a smile as he saw Menon and Maakan at his gate.

THE RETURN

The air had the same sweetness. The trees sang the same songs as before. He felt lucky. So often, you return to your childhood only to find everything changed. Not for him. Not here. He knew that he was being selfish. After all, he had been away for more than three decades. He was no longer the scrawny teen who roamed these roads. He no longer slurped his tea from a bowl nor had ice cream with biscuit toppings. He could no longer flip a flat pebble across the water five times in a row or aim straight at the mangoes in the nearby orchard. He had changed, but he did not want his childhood to be altered. This place should be the same, he believed.

The path curved as it always did near the river. The breeze brought the same fragrance as before. He craned his neck in anticipation. Yes, there was the jambul tree or the black plum. The gate to the house looked freshly painted. Whoever lived there took good care of it. He entered the compound and frowned. The swing had disappeared, and a tiny house stood on the same sturdy branch that reached out horizontally across the yard.

A tree-house? They built a tree house on his favourite tree! He felt a rage building inside as he scrambled to the wooden box with tiny windows. In a corner stood a stool with a stack of toy boxes nearby. A mattress with a blanket and a pillow lay near a window. He looked out through the window.

The branch stretched like a brown cylindrical pathway. He had reached the end of the tether. At the end of the branch, he saw the end of the world as he knew. He closed his eyes to savour the moment. Then jumped. A rope appeared in his hand and a plank broad enough to seat a person. He swung the plank over the branch and jumped down with the two ends of the rope. He tightened the knots and then tested the swing. Up, up in the air, he went. It was bliss.

"It is time," said a voice from the branches.

He nodded. He knew. The wound on the head had begun to ache. His leg was already frozen, and his heartbeat was slow.

"You had your last wish. Let's go," said the voice.

He took one last look at his childhood home, then said a final goodbye.

S.O.S

"This is not about saving our planet; it's about saving ourselves. The truth is, with or without us, the natural world will rebuild."

– David Attenborough

FLOOD. RINSE. DRAIN. REPEAT.

The car swayed when the adjacent bus made soft, murky waves on the four-lane road. Vinu gripped the steering wheel tighter. He twisted his neck to look up at the bus driver and recoiled. The driver stared like a deer caught in the headlights of an oncoming car, eyes round and dazed.

Mumbai, trapped in a torrent with its relentless drumming, pouring, and flooding, scared even its hardiest residents.

The dashboard rang. "Mom, where are you?"

"We are on our way," a terrified voice emerged from the passenger seat beside Vinu. He did not dare look at the mousy form of his wife. Reenu froze when she saw two buses coming towards them. The waves that formed were not as benign as before. The car rocked.

"The city is drowning. Get out of there, guys."

Vinu smiled despite the situation. Mini was safe. She dragged out the 'guys' whenever she wanted to tease her parents. She appeared relaxed. That is all that mattered. On the other hand, a visceral fear emanated from the passenger seat.

"How are you all holding up?" he asked, turning to the dashboard.

"We are fine, Dad. Get out of there as fast as you can." Their daughter's voice floated through the car's thick, synthetically fragranced air.

Vinu took a deep breath. "I am trying," he said, but he wasn't sure if his words reached before the call disconnected. He squinted as he saw a human form moving towards the car. A man in a black raincoat and yellow swimming cap waded through the murky waters. The two buses had stopped in the middle of the cloudy pool.

The man gestured as he moved closer. This solitary man's slow, tired legs created ripples big enough to tilt the car.

Vinu opened the window just enough to let his voice through as the man approached. "Sir, how is it ahead? Can we proceed?"

The man shook his head and then yelled to throw his voice above the din of the incessant rain. "Leave the car and go!" he pointed in the direction he had walked from. "Leave and go!" he repeated. This time, his gestures were frantic.

Vinu looked at his wife for the first time after leaving home two hours ago. She nodded. "Let's go."

As he turned the key, Reenu handed him his backpack. He turned around to look at the luggage in the backseat. There was one large suitcase and another bag in the boot with clothes and some books, but the ones in the back contained food, whatever they could carry from what was left at home and in the fridge.

Reenu shook her head. "Not possible, Vinu." Her eyes probed the dark waters that lay ahead of them. "The water is rising!"

"Can't we give it to someone in need?"

Reenu jabbed her finger at the window. “Look, Vinu, look! We won’t be able to walk even a few feet with those heavy bags.”

She was right.

Vinu took a deep breath and opened the door. He felt his socks absorbing the wetness. He made his way to the other side and let her out.

They both gave one longing look at their car and began their trek through the waters.

It was not the first time that they had abandoned their car. They knew the drill. Insurance, claims, hopeful assurances from the car company that they could repair the vehicle, and the final blow when they insist it is only worth the scrap.

Vinu and Reenu kept to the middle of the road; their hands clasped. There were no tell-tale eddies to indicate open manholes, but who could tell if a cover was missing in such a downpour? The aftermath of an open hole would be inconspicuous. Who would notice bodies swept into the open seas? Relatives would lodge a missing person complaint, and if they were lucky, their bodies might wash up on some shore.

Reenu shuddered at the thought.

“You should have worn another jacket,” Vinu said.

“I am wearing three layers.”

“Right! Any more and you might topple our car with the waves you create,” Vinu grinned.

Reenu let out a tiny chuckle despite the fears lurking in her mind. Trust Vinu to keep his sense of humour intact.

The phone rang inside Vinu's pocket. He couldn't afford losing his phone in this heavy downpour. He let it ring.

"Why aren't they picking up the phone?" Mini winced as her agitated hand caught the edge of the table.

Shyamala looked at her husband, Krishnan, for help, but he was focused on turning the dusty old radio knobs this way and that to catch some signal. Miraculously, the ancient relic stuttered and stammered before it belted out an old classic. For a moment, Krishnan forgot why he fiddled with the radio. The song took him back to the good old days until Mini called out. "Grandpa, any news?" He continued to tune into any radio channel with news on the floods.

It was not an isolated event in one part of the country. Nearly the entire subcontinent was covered by a thick blanket of clouds in the satellite picture carried by the newspaper yesterday.

Krishnan's house was at a location higher than the sea level, so they were safe for now. Mini had joined them soon after her campus flooded and earlier than her vacation officially began. She came home to her grandparents with a weary and dejected look. "We wanted to help in every way we could. The shanties outside our campus were carried away by the floodwaters. We accommodated the residents in our hostels. We could have done more, but the college management asked us to return home."

"It was the right decision. Food and water might be in short supply. If there are less people on the campus, they can focus on those actually in need," Shyamala had consoled her.

Mini spent two days at her grandparents' house in nervous anticipation of the havoc the floods might create in the city. And then the news arrived: the city was drowning.

Now at her grandparent's home, Mini tried her dad's phone for the twentieth time. "They should have left the same day when I reached here. I kept telling them to be alert."

"Where were they when you last spoke?" Krishnan asked suddenly. He had picked up some locations in the news on the radio, places that sounded familiar.

"They didn't mention. Why? What's wrong?"

Mini moved closer to the radio when Krishnan didn't reply. A chill crept through her feet and up to her heart. The residents were up on the roofs, asking for help. The water had cut off a few localities. One of the localities was theirs.

She gulped and started ringing up with more anxious vigour.

Meanwhile, her parents waded through the flooded roads. They had no clue what lay ahead. Buses stood stranded in the middle of the lanes. Passengers balanced themselves on the top of the buses.

Reenu shuddered to imagine a scenario if the bus were to topple. She tried to move away from the bus.

"What are you doing?" Vinu hissed. "Keep to the centre of the road."

She shot a scared look at Vinu.

"Do you realise that this is perhaps the longest we have held hands in the past few years?" he asked.

Reenu smirked. "What a romantic scene!" she exclaimed, pointing to the dark grey water surrounding them.

"In good times and bad!" Vinu exclaimed.

That evoked a smile from Reenu. "She must be distraught now," she said after a while. She yearned to hear Mini's voice.

Vinu focused his attention on the road. He could see more people a few hundred metres ahead. That could mean two things: either a mishap had occurred or the lay of the land was rising, making the floodwaters shallow.

A few kilometres away, Mini heard more updates on the radio. "If they can reach this railway station, she pointed to a map on her mobile phone, then I think they can find a way out."

"But there are no trains," Shyamala objected.

"They can walk. They will walk," Krishnan replied. His belief proved to be correct.

An hour later, a breathless Vinu called to notify them that they had reached the railway station and the roads beyond it were better off. The tracks were flooded, but they were walking along a parallel street. They were wet, but the water was only a few inches.

Mini sighed in relief and flopped down on the sofa. She toyed with a steel glass in which her grandmother had offered her some black tea. There was no milk in the house.

"Black tea is good for health," Krishnan said as he observed Mini. "Now, if we had Pediasure—"

Mini looked at her grandfather, and they both started laughing.

"What is the joke?" Shyamala asked. She was still a bit shaken by the turn of events.

She only hoped that all their phones had enough charge so that they could get updates from her children.

"Didn't I tell you about when we had Pediasure three times a day?" Krishnan asked, doubling up in laughter.

Shyamala recollected the incident as narrated by her husband. "Nothing to laugh about," she scoffed. "Reenu had a good presence of mind."

"Yes, but that's not the point," Krishnan said. "It was... it was..." But now that he thought about it, he couldn't remember what was so funny.

"It was the candle, Grandpa!" Mini said with a chuckle.

"Aah, yes, the candle!"

"What was that?" Shyamala asked.

"So, this was during the 2015 Chennai floods. We had no power and no gas supply."

"I remember. It was because they had all the gas cylinders on the ground floor and claimed to have piped gas supply." Shyamala shook her head in indignation.

"But that's how it is in many modern apartments, Grandma."

"Well, because we didn't have a gas supply and the milk had gone bad, Reenu used a candle to heat a steel tumbler with water and mixed Pediasure into it. She did this patiently for every person, one at a time, three times a day!" Krishnan continued with a guffaw.

A flash of lightning lit up the hall, followed immediately by a thunder crash. Mini shuddered as she huddled onto her chair. "I still don't like thunderstorms," she grimaced.

"You managed quite well for an eight-year-old," Krishnan reminisced. "Thank God you were not there, Shyamala. You would have driven us mad."

"Do you know how anxious we were? We couldn't contact you or anyone in the city." Shyamala accused. "No one to help you out. Just you, Reenu, and Mini. If you did not have that conference, it would have been just Reenu and Mini. Imagine!"

Krishnan ignored the outburst. "Do you remember jumping across the parapet walls, Mini?"

"I do. I was carrying Mom's laptop."

"Such a tiny child, carrying a laptop?" Shyamala was aghast.

"Each of us had a bag to carry," Krishnan reminded. "Besides, we should be thankful that all the building blocks were connected. Imagine if they were all separate. We would have been stranded on the terrace."

"And I remember the food. It was so tasty!" Mini added.

"The food? We didn't get any, remember? Good Samaritans would send the message that they had arranged for food. Reenu would jump over four parapet walls to reach there only to return empty-handed because the food was over," Krishnan looked at Shyamala as he spoke.

"It was a shame because even the scraps in the vessels gave off such a delicious scent as we passed it. Remember? I think that's what I recollect. The smell, not the taste. We saw the vessels when we reached the first block to get onto the boat," Mini corrected herself.

"Aah, yes, I remember seeing the vessels, but you have such a keen memory of smell," he smiled appreciatively at Mini.

"You said others were waiting along with you." Shyamala tried to recollect from Krishnan's accounts.

"Yes, there were two other families. One with a tiny child, less than a year old. The family looked terrified."

"That water could have terrified anyone, Grandma. Imagine looking out your window and seeing just a grey expanse in the sky and below. Do you remember how it looked on normal days? We could see the sun dip into the marsh, the vehicles blinking from the highway beyond, and the lights from the office buildings. I always felt proud that Mom worked in one of those offices." Mini smiled as she reminisced. "And then, we could only see the water rising for three consecutive nights. All we could hear were the frogs croaking and the dogs howling."

"Eerie!" Shyamala agreed.

"Do you remember the cycle?" Krishnan asked.

"Yes!" Mini replied with a chuckle. "There was a cycle leaning against the wall in the parking lot. We could see it from the balcony. That was Grandpa's water level marker," she explained to Shyamala.

"I pointed it out to her only once, and then she would look at it every hour to check if the water level was changing," he chuckled, pointing to Mini.

"We were so tensed. There was no way into the city," Shyamala recounted.

"You know, in 2005, I used a measuring tape to track the rising level," Krishnan said, ignoring Shyamala.

"That's a huge difference, a measuring tape in Mumbai 2005 and a cycle in Chennai 2015. It could well be a bus this year," Mini muttered.

She was on the phone again. There had been no updates from her parents for the last fifteen minutes.

"They're not picking up," she said.

"They'll call when they are in a better position. Give them some time," Krishnan said gently. He glanced at Shyamala. "We would have called, too, but we were worried about the power supply. We were charging our phones using our laptops."

Shyamala nodded. It was an explanation that made sense today but did little to quell the anxiety on that fateful day in 2015.

"Why don't you tell us about the measuring tape, Grandpa? It wouldn't have been as bad as this."

"It was. The city was cut off. However, I was alone at home," he paused as he recollected, "until the rains started pouring heavily. Then my colleague joined me as he couldn't go home."

"Thank God for that," Shyamala remarked. "Or else, you would have been alone at home when the waters gushed in. I was stuck at the office."

"She had to spend her night at her workplace," Krishnan added. "I was glad she was not on the road. Cars, autos, and scooters were carried away by the floods. Our local bank branch manager got washed away. They found his car thirty kilometres away in the creek. He couldn't get out in time."

Shyamala exchanged glances with Mini. "They have abandoned their car, Grandma. Don't worry," Mini said, nodding at Shyamala.

"But what she said is right," Krishnan continued, not noticing the exchange between Mini and Shyamala. "The waters gushed in. I had closed all the doors and windows. The TV was on, I remember. I went to the kitchen and saw the weirdest thing ever. Dozens of cockroaches ran out of the drain pipes. I had never seen so many of them scampering around the place. It was annoying at first, but later I got terrified. It was like an omen, a sign of an apocalypse. They ran as if their house was on fire. Except, it was not fire but water. I saw drops of water spurting out of the drain like someone blowing bubbles. I went to investigate, but as I neared the window, the noise intensified. It was not the white noise of a steady downpour. There was something else happening outside. I remember opening the veranda door and experiencing something I had never seen before. The force of the water gushing in nearly toppled me. It was the marsh. It was overflowing."

"Do you remember, Grandpa, how the compound wall of our apartment had sprung leaks? It was again the marsh that was overflowing," Mini asked.

"Yes, but they said it was due to the untimely opening of the reservoir gates."

"Untimely and un-warned, perhaps," Mini replied with a smirk.

"But the one in 2005 was not that. It was simply the marsh overflowing," Krishnan countered.

"Did it ever happen before they built the road across it?" Shyamala asked.

"No, it was the first time," Krishnan acknowledged.

"While building the road, they dumped debris into the marsh. I am sure they blocked the stormwater drains," Shyamala added, looking at Mini.

"It's always the marsh, isn't it? The wetlands. They protect us, but now they need protection." Mini pondered. Then, remembering her question, she asked, "But the measuring tape?"

"Yes, so the gushing water gave us little time. We tried to get as many things off the floor as possible. Uday, my friend, even wanted to see if we could get the books out of the lower shelves of the cupboard. But it was too late for that."

"If I were there, I would have removed the photo albums. We lost several of our college photos. They didn't come laminated in those days, only stuck on a piece of cardboard," Shyamala complained.

"We sat on the chairs with our feet pulled up. We sat the whole night in that manner. Those days, my knees were stronger. I can't think of pulling them up like that now."

"I remember Grandpa, your knees troubled you while jumping over the parapet during the 2015 floods," Mini recollected.

"Yes, and that is why your mother was adamant that we should go to the first block only after ensuring the rescue boat arrived as expected. I couldn't go jumping across walls multiple times."

"So, in 2005, you sat with your legs folded up on the chair?" Mini urged him to continue.

"We sat like that for eight hours. I dipped the measuring tape in the water to see if it changed. It did not go down but did not rise either, which was a relief. If not the chair, the next option was the dining table, then the kitchen platform, and after that..."

"Thank God the water receded in the morning," Shyamala interrupted to avoid the exploration of morbid possibilities.

"Yes, the water started receding by five a.m. When your grandmother arrived in the morning, she was shocked to see the state of the house."

"It was like a paddy field with dirt and mud everywhere. But I was relieved to be home. The taxi driver who ferried us was terrified. We were scared, too. There were animal carcasses everywhere on the road, including buffaloes with swollen bodies," Shyamala shuddered involuntarily. "I had not seen such scenes even in the movies."

She pointed at Krishnan before continuing, "When I came home, your grandfather was trying to clean up the mess inside the house. His colleague had left as soon as the water level came down. There was no power supply, just like now. And we didn't even have candles."

"I remember queuing up at the local Kirana shop for candles," Krishnan said with a chuckle.

"How much time did it take to clean the house?" Mini asked curiously.

"A week!" Krishnan and Shyamala replied in unison, smiling.

"Cleaning our one-room tenement was easier, wasn't it?" Shyamala asked, punctuating her question with a laugh.

"Yes. We did that nearly every day during monsoons," Krishnan replied with a nod and a smile.

"When was that?" Mini asked.

"Look at the steel tumbler in your hand. Can you read anything?" Shyamala asked. Her eyes twinkled with delight.

"There is a year engraved on it, 1977. Probably a month, too."

"That was the year your father was born. This steel tumbler was a gift to the new-born. It was the twenty-eighth-day celebration. We organised a lunch for our friends. A proper sit-down lunch with banana leaves and all, but the monsoon had other plans. We had torrential rains that day, and water seeped into our room in the chawl. We spent half the day sweeping the water out with a broom and pail." Shyamala reminisced.

Krishnan guffawed. "It was a good thing that everyone was hungry. Despite the wet weather, they wolfed down everything we prepared. Cleaning the room was easy because it was a plain, flat surface that sloped towards a drain at the end of the room. So, we just poured water from the storage drums. The irony was that we faced a water shortage for the next few days despite the rains. One day of flooding, cleaning, and feasting, two days of no water to drink, cook or bathe."

Mini gaped. "What did you do?"

"I don't remember, actually," Shyamala said with an uneasy laugh.

"Yes, we didn't even have Pediasure, did we?" Krishnan asked, bursting into an uproar.

"I think we didn't have anything left in our pantry, but we were never stressed out," Shyamala smiled. "At least, I don't remember feeling stressed."

Just then, the doorbell rang. Mini flew to open the door. "Dad! Mom!" she screamed as she saw them.

Vinu and Reenu stood at the door with sheepish grins. The tryst with the storm showed on their clothes. "We hitched a ride with a group in a tempo traveller."

Shyamala instinctively went to light a lamp at her tiny temple. "It is midnight, Shyamala. Don't do that now. Light the lamp bright and early in the morning," Krishnan reminded her.

Vinu and Reenu slumped on the floor, exhausted.

"So, the car's gone?" Mini eyed them mischievously.

"This is not the first time, is it?" Reenu asked. They had abandoned their car in 2015 in their flooded ground floor parking as they clambered into the rescue boats to drier spots.

"Do you realise how many floods we have been through as a family?" Mini asked, looking around. "And across cities, too."

Everyone nodded, albeit in trepidation. "Every flood has been more vicious than before," Vinu said slowly. "What if the next one is like nothing we have ever seen?"

Outside, the rain continued to pour. Inside, the stories followed the rhythm of nature— flood, rinse, drain, repeat.

THE LAST RESORT

The aircraft shuddered, afraid to test the stability of the ground, as it landed on the tarmac. A similar tremble went through Sandy as he scanned the areas around the airport. The services had resumed after fifteen days of closure due to inclement weather. Three days of turbulent storms and flooded airports made it hard to reopen.

The remnants of the floods could still be seen on the water-swept grounds outside the airport premises. Nature's fury had painted the land with broad strokes of brown shades. Beige icky mud from the nearby river that suddenly proclaimed its existence after years of strangulation by the city dwellers coated the landscape. Choked of its passage to the sea, the river rose to the occasion and swept away man's misdeeds.

Sandy muttered a prayer for the suffering masses as he walked out of the arrivals area. A few taxi drivers hung around, driven more by their self-preservation than the safety of the passengers who travelled under uncertain circumstances. Sandy found one who looked trustworthy and flagged the booking receipt to him. The driver looked at the destination printed on the thin wad of paper. "I hope you don't have a train to catch in the next three hours. We aren't going to reach before that."

Sandy waved his hand. "My train is at midnight."

As they navigated the rubble-filled roads, Sandy made a quick call. "Did you find out? Is the place still available?"

"Sir, don't worry. I'll take care of everything. You'll be here by tomorrow afternoon, right?"

"Yes, yes."

"Alright then. See you tomorrow."

When Sandy kept away the phone, the driver spoke up.

"You here to buy property?"

Sandy did not reply.

"My neighbour's son also works abroad. He has invested in an apartment in the city."

Sandy nodded. His thoughts went to his beachfront villa not far from the city. He sold it last year at a throwaway price. The sea swallowed half of the property.

"Many people working abroad like to invest here. I am thinking of doing a side business as a real estate agent," the driver said with a chuckle.

Sandy had made his broker promise him a deal within two days. He was desperate. His chances were dwindling.

"Why don't they buy abroad where they live?" the driver asked, genuinely curious.

"Lot of problems. Visa, citizenship, sometimes prices are too high. Different countries, different challenges," Sandy tried to explain.

The taxi driver chuckled. "I thought money could get you a home anywhere."

Sandy gave a bitter smile as the memories from two years ago poked new holes into his confidence. A dream house in a distant land engulfed in a forest fire. He had insurance, fortunately. But it was a ten-year-old household that had burned down to ashes. They started again with great vigour yet struggled to regain confidence in the land.

"I have a small house in my village," the driver continued. "High in the mountains, but I haven't checked on it for years."

"Leased it to someone?" Sandy asked, intrigued. The driver nodded.

"A family friend, so I can trust him."

Sandy sighed. Their vacation house was high up in the mountains on a scarp. A landslide caused half of the scarp to fall away. Looking at the precarious situation, local authorities warned him about the dangers of living in the house. "But we don't live here." Sandy's admission did not sit well with the locals.

"The house can pose a danger to others in the village," a local leader proclaimed. Sandy turned to his wife, who shrugged. "Mountains are no longer safe," she remarked sorrowfully.

This was five years before they purchased the beachfront property in their home country. The mountaintop house was their first foreign investment. And now, he only wanted a place to call his own anywhere, somewhere on this planet.

A tiny house with a mango tree in its backyard. A swing on the porch. A well in its front yard. Guava and cashewnut trees jostling for space beside the mango tree. He reminisced how he would run around the empty spaces in his mother's garden, careful not to trample on her flower beds.

The phone rang, jolting him out of his reverie. "Sir, Will you be interested in another place?"

"What? No! I told you I want the same place."

"Sir, that is prime locality now. They have sold it already to a resort chain."

Sandy sighed and closed his eyes. Where on earth will he find his last resort?

THAT SINKING FEELING

Kailas ignored the pleading eyes that followed him as he stepped out for his morning jog. Every morning, he had to suffer torturous stares.

A man set up a makeshift snacks stall across the road two months ago. Kailas had purchased the snacks once from him. Since then, the man's eyes followed him every time he passed by. He yearned to taste the snacks once more but the pleading eyes made him anxious.

The snacks were pure nostalgia, the same taste from his childhood when his mother made them for him and his siblings. She stopped making them when they moved to a new country. It was not her fault that Kailas and his siblings moved on to more contemporary foods. They preferred the flavours of their adopted home, where two of his siblings were born.

Like his parents and elder sister, Kailas's birthplace was a tiny island off the mainland. His father sought more affluent shores after Kailas turned five.

"The island is sinking," his father used to remind. "We need to get away as soon as we can."

Once they reached the mainland, life started afresh. His father was a qualified doctor and set up his own practice. His mother was an economical homemaker, and the children benefitted from their parents' attitude towards education. They grew up respecting hard work and ambitions. Kailas took over his father's practice and the modest house. He had forgotten his old island until last month when he tasted the homemade snacks at the roadside stall.

The stall owner appeared familiar yet strange. His sorrowful eyes reminded Kailas of a long-lost yearning for clean, open beaches, salty air, and carefree days. An unexpected sinking feeling inhabited his stomach. The island that had floated away from his memories now loomed large in his dreams. It disturbed Kailas because along with those dreams came recollections of friends and neighbours they had left behind.

"Papa!" Kailas's daughter Anika, entering his study, called out with uncharacteristic excitement. He looked up at the teen in surprise. A brooding silence usually greeted him when he wished her every morning, so this was something big.

"Did you know that Uncle Jamaal is also from Ranidweepa?"

"Who's Jamaal?"

Anika shook her head. "You are the one who bought those oily snacks from him last month."

"I bought them just once." Kailas defended his transgression from the healthy diet standards set by his wife and daughter. Sometimes, he felt his medical degree was merely a prop in his consulting room. His family, with no such educational background, offered more medical advice than him.

"Well, good for you," Anika said with a wry smile. "But you should talk to him. What if he knew Grandpa?"

Kailas went back to his book with a half-hearted nod. Now, Anika would keep at it until he spoke to Jamaal. Taking her to the local museum to teach her about Ranidweepa had been a mistake. He had done it a few years ago in a sudden rush of homesickness. A local news channel reported about shrinking beaches and sinking houses in Ranidweepa. The island was on the verge of being swallowed by the sea. Something that his father had always warned about was now becoming true.

"Pa?" Kailas was surprised Anika had not left the room.

"Yes?"

"I have to tell you something."

"What?"

"I lent Uncle some money."

"What?!"

"He is in dire need of cash to pay his children's school fees."

"Anika, that doesn't help him. It'll eventually do him more harm. He has to earn a living."

"Yes! That's exactly why I want you to speak to him. If he can't earn a living here, he'll have to get onto a boat back to the island."

Kailas shook his head. "He should have thought twice before becoming a refugee."

"Pa," Anika's voice took a grim undertone. "No one decides to become a refugee. Grandpa left the island. Why?"

"He had said Ranidweepa was sinking. But he planned his migration."

"Grandpa and Uncle Jamaal were worried about the sinking ship, but they were not rats to abandoned it.

They were only protecting their families. The only difference is Grandpa migrated while Uncle Jamaal sought refuge."

Kailas inhaled the moist sea breeze through the open window. "The sea doesn't differentiate between migrants or refugees. Everyone's home gets swallowed if they aren't careful," he mumbled, hoping Anika didn't hear.

But she had. "Yes, Pa, but we must know the difference because not everyone can afford a new home. Their home was sinking."

Kailas stepped out to meet Jamaal because he knew that sinking feeling.

NANBAN

The camera disappeared first, and then the hands that held them. Pralob winced as he saw the head behind the camera vanish right after. His grimace turned into a gasp as he ran towards the rock. Where did that cheeky boy go? With his heart in his mouth, he clambered up the rock and peered over. The boy crouched below with a grin on his face. Both he and the camera were safe. Pralob let out a sigh of relief. "What do you think you—?"

"Quiet!" the boy placed a finger on his lips, then pointed ahead.

Pralob's eyes followed the direction and observed the most beautiful sight. A kaleidoscope of yellows flitted among the shrubs, creating a bright, moving tapestry on a wall of green.

The boy held the camera precisely how he had seen Pralob do a while ago and clicked. He then handed the camera to Pralob and climbed back over the rock. Pralob nodded at the photo. "You are a fast learner. I'll frame this before I go back to America." The boy beamed with pride.

"And now, shall we proceed?" Pralob asked impatiently.

The boy skipped ahead in response and gestured to follow him. "Why do you want to go there?" he asked.

"To click more pictures," Pralob replied absentmindedly. His gaze was fixed on the valley below. Dense with vegetation and trees, there was hardly a gap through which he could gauge the depth.

"What were you doing at that rock when I saw you first?" Pralob asked the boy, his voice muffled behind the camera as he positioned himself for a click of the valley. The boy remained mesmerised by Pralob's actions. "Hello?" Pralob prompted after he had clicked the picture.

"What?"

"What were you doing when I saw you?"

"I was hiding from Nanban."

"Ha-ha! Nanban! Is he still around?"

The boy grinned, flashing his white teeth with surprising frankness. "The legend says so."

"What do you know about Nanban?" Pralob teased the boy.

The boy flashed his toothy grin again. "Everything my grandmother told me."

Pralob shook his head. "Stories tend to grow as they are told and retold. Especially when it's about someone as mysterious as Nanban."

The boy frowned, unable to comprehend.

"What did your grandmother tell you?"

"That I would have to face Nanban if I did anything wrong by the jungle."

Pralob's eyes twinkled with mischief as he looked at the boy, "And what have you done?"

The boy hung his head in silence.

"Go on. It'll be our secret. I won't tell anyone."

The boy looked squarely into Pralob's eyes. After pondering for a while, he decided that Pralob could be trusted. "I threw a plastic bottle into the waterfall. I wanted to see how far it goes, and I was always going to pick it up downstream, but I couldn't find it when I went below the rocks… and… and…"

"Hush!" Pralob shook the boy by his shoulders. "Calm down! You threw a bottle into the water. What's the big deal?"

The boy looked at Pralob in astonishment. "Don't you know it's against the rules?"

"What rules? Whose rules?"

"The rules of nature, set by our Devi and followed by all of us. Nanban guards the jungle. If anyone does anything against nature, he'll punish them."

Pralob scoffed. "Who told you all this nonsense?" He chuckled, then kicked a twig out of his way.

"Stupid rules!" He climbed ahead of the boy, who looked at him in confusion.

"Wait! Wait for me!" As the boy caught up with Pralob, a crumbling structure loomed ahead, a simple, single-storeyed building with walls made of stone.

Pralob stopped dead in his tracks and was so taken up by what he saw that he forgot to click a picture on his camera. Instead, he stood there, gaping at the structure.

The boy observed Pralob and the building in turns. "Is this what you were looking for, the old village school?" Pralob did not answer, but the boy realised the place was important. "Also, these are not stupid rules. They keep the jungle clean.

"Huh?" Pralob stumbled out of his reverie.

"Our rules? You said they are stupid. They are not. It keeps the place clean. My teacher at school said so."

Pralob did not react. He was in a daze. With a stupefied expression, he opened the half-broken door and entered. Inside was a single classroom with a blackboard painted on the wall, broken desks, and benches strewn around. The place smelled musty, and the dust lay thick on the floor and every piece of furniture. Pralob went straight to the back of the classroom. He rubbed off some dust from the wall with his bare hands. The boy gasped when he saw what Pralob had uncovered.

"Nanban!" he whispered.

Pralob nodded in response. "The real one, not the legend."

The boy frowned, and then he saw something, the letter P, near the spotted tail of the leopard. "P for?"

"Pralob."

The boy's frown deepened. "You knew Nanban."

Pralob nodded. "I saw him. I drew him. When I was your age."

The boy's frown turned into a scowl. "What did you do to make Nanban appear before you?"

Pralob looked the boy in the eye as if to say sorry. "I led the bad men into the jungle."

"The ones who destroyed the sacred hill a decade ago?"

Pralob nodded.

“The ones who wanted to cut down the trees in our jungles?” the boy’s voice had gained pitch and intensity.

Pralob sighed.

“The ones who killed Nanban?” the boy nearly shrieked.

Pralob pursed his lips and stared at the boy.

The boy looked as if he was about to spit insults at Pralob, but his anger turned to fright as he heard a sharp growl. He crouched under the desk. Pralob instinctively jumped out of the window.

“The rules are not stupid,” the boy whispered as he spied a spotted feline figure following Pralob.

OUTSIDE THE WINDOW

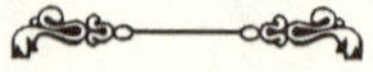

The man glared at the monstrosity outside his window.

A gigantic grey lumpen trunk with a dirty green, overgrown mane blocked his view of the city. He abhorred it. The birds inhabiting its branches treated his outdoor patio like a lavatory; their droppings caused pockmarks on its immaculate tiles. The dead leafy garbage strewn from the tree's upper echelons created constant work for his cleaners.

The tree blocked the light coming into his hall. He turned to look at the million-dollar painting strategically placed to impress his guests into silence as they entered. In the meagre light falling through the windows, it was a pale shadow of itself. The man sighed as he switched on the focus lights mid-morning. The monster outside marred his share of the sunlight.

And the swing! Gosh! The swing! It made his heart beat wildly whenever he saw his boy on it. It could be dangerous.

Across the hall, in the adjacent room, a boy gazed at one of nature's most beautiful creations. Sturdy, smooth, and grey, with a glossy green crown, it majestically watched over their home. He loved it. Its bitter-sweet fruits fell like tiny drops of joy just for him. The leaves blowing in the wind created a soft shower on breezy afternoons. He loved walking over the beautiful carpet they spread on the patio.

The chinks in its foliage drew intricate designs on the wall in his room. It was a play of shadow and light, symmetry created by randomness, artwork by nature worth all the lonely mornings he spent in bed, gazing at the wall.

And the swing! Gosh! The swing! It made his heart beat wildly whenever he was on it. It was thrilling.

The man with the machine came in the afternoon. The clanging of the chain and the choppy whir of the saw disturbed the household siesta. The thundering thud as the majestic tree crashed to the ground brought the father and son to their windows.

The father had a smug smile. He was tired of travelling and wished to live peacefully in his grand and palatial house. He got rid of the one thing he hated about it.

The boy had tears. He was heartbroken and wished to run far away from home. He lost the one thing he loved about it.

A WORLD UNSEEN

"There are two ways of spreading light: to be the candle or the mirror that reflects it."

– *Edith Wharton*

A DREAM

Under the mellow sun, Vishal wiped off the sweat on his brow and adjusted the carton on his motorcycle seat. One order remained. Looking at the address again, he recalled the familiar route but failed to recognise the locality.

The landmark was a well-known four-star hotel. Opposite the hotel was a cafe from where Vishal and his friends often ogled at the cars plying through its gates. The vehicles offered them a glimpse into a possible future, a realisation of their colourful dreams.

Vishal was the only one among his friends who did not divulge his aspirations. He was embarrassed of his low-brow ambitions. While his friends spoke about five-figure salaries, he dreamed of starting a spare parts business. The job as a delivery guy was a stop-gap arrangement before he could amass some capital.

Vishal passed by the cafe and turned into the alley to deliver the last order for the day. His bike rode into a world far removed from the glamour that shone from the resplendent hotel windows. The locality became shabbier as he passed low-roofed houses, built cheek by jowl. The faces that peered out of them turned scrawnier.

After a point, he couldn't go further unless he rode over someone's foot or bumped into a front door. So, he parked his motorcycle and walked with the package in hand. He was doubtful about the address. It merely said, Sayali Jyoti,

Room no 34, Ganesh Pakhadi. A delivery like this could prove to be a headache. To his surprise, he saw a signboard in the local language that read - Way to Sayali's house.

Never before had he seen an addressee's house being identified in such a way.

Vishal knocked on the door. It was opened by an octogenarian woman. A nervous middle-aged woman stood behind her.

"I have a parcel for Sayali?" he queried for the receiver.

The old woman stretched out her hands and accepted the package. She was so frail that the box dwarfed her petite body. She nearly lost her balance.

"Keep it on the floor, Grandma," a sweet yet firm voice floated from the other end of the room.

"Till now, she received only flowers. Now they have started sending parcels, too. Wonder what this is?" said the middle-aged lady as she shook the parcel and started unpacking.

"Sorry, Aunty," Vishal said, "I need to go now. Can somebody sign on this paper?" he asked.

Both the women looked towards the corner of the room, where that sweet voice had spoken earlier.

Vishal stretched out the paper in his hand.

The grandmother looked at him. "Come in."

In the light of the solitary bulb in the room, Vishal saw a girl lying on a makeshift bed. Her head was bandaged, and her right hand was held up in plaster. She tried to sit up but could not do so without tremendous difficulty.

Vishal stood aside while her mother ran forward to help her. As she pulled her daughter up, the bed linen covering the lower part of her torso slipped away, revealing a bandaged and bloodied stump. The sight of blood rattled him, and he froze.

The mother snatched the paper from him and took it to her daughter, who signed with great flourish.

"Here. Drink some water," said the grandmother, bringing him out of his trance. He drank the water without a word. When the mother returned with the paper, he was outside the door but burning with curiosity.

"What happened?" he asked in a puzzled tone. It seemed that he was not the first one to ask.

The mother sighed but had her answer ready. 'She lost her leg in a scuffle."

Vishal couldn't believe his ears. The girl was barely a teenager. And she lost her leg in a fight? "A fight?" he asked somewhat stupidly.

The mother took a deep breath.

"I guess you want to hear the complete story now. Come inside. Too many mosquitoes here. I don't want to keep the door open."

Vishal stepped inside again and, this time, found that the girl was looking at him with interest.

The bed linen was arranged so that Vishal could not see the stump. The mother narrated their story.

The three of them lived by themselves. The older women went to work while Sayali studied at the local school.

When the grandmother fell ill and could not work, they borrowed money from a local loan shark.

“I defaulted on a few payments. The man sent his men down to threaten us. Sayali had just come back from school. She asked them to leave, but they entered by force. She pushed a man out. He got angry and pulled her out with him. When he heard her yelling at our neighbour to call the police, he hit her several times with a rod and threw her into the gutter. Something sharp pierced into her leg and wounded her. We took her to the hospital, but they delayed the treatment; finally, her leg had to be amputated. A few organisations came forward claiming that they could help us. Some reporters also came!” she waved her hand dismissively.

“They ran a story in the local newspapers. Since then, we have been getting flowers and bouquets. People find it difficult to find our house, so I got some boys to fix up the board outside.”

Vishal looked at the half-opened parcel. It was a big teddy bear.

“This does not help, does it?” She asked nonchalantly and then rose. It was his cue to leave.

But Vishal was not satisfied. He kept thinking about Sayali on his way home. He had aspirations and dreams. Wouldn’t Sayali have them, too?

In the following days, he found and visited the doctor treating Sayali and enquired about the future course of action. He learned that Sayali should be able to walk on crutches soon, but her medical bills were pending. Vishal dipped into his savings account to pay Sayali's medical bills and ensure her treatment continued.

He approached an NGO through his friend to get legal aid for Sayali. On weekends, he became a regular at Sayali's house to help her prepare for the exams. Sayali, in turn, encouraged him to get a degree.

After a few months, Vishal got together with his friends at their usual haunt, the cafe right outside the four-star hotel. However, when he looked at the cars going by this time, he was thinking about another set of wheels lying in a shed behind his house-- an automated wheelchair that he designed, keeping Sayali in mind.

"Can wheelchairs be sold online?" he asked no one in particular, a shy smile breaking across his face as he finally shared his dream.

THE GOLDEN SHOWER

The gong pierced through the hazy city that never sleeps. Arun stepped out of the factory compound in a daze.

The last hour of his shift squeezed every ounce of energy from his famished body. A half glass of thick sweetened milk tea and a piece of bun sustained him for the last three hours. He dragged his weary feet to the bus stop.

The backpack with a pair of clothes hung heavy on his shoulders. After the shift, he had not bothered to exchange his uniform for his day clothes. All he needed now was a quick bath in the shared bathroom in his dormitory, provided none of the other nine occupants were using it, and then hit the bed like a sack of potatoes. And potatoes, there were plenty in his system. The only vegetable he could afford to eat on a working day.

Arun looked at his watch. Heck! He had missed the last bus home. He looked longingly at the half-covered bus stop bench. The choice was between letting his sleep overcome all reasoning to risk being awakened by a policeman's stick or walking along the lonely railway tracks for the shortest way to the dormitory.

The policeman appeared around the corner, forcing a prompt decision. He veered into the opening in the hedges and jumped gingerly onto the narrow space between the shrubs and the tracks. If a train whooshes by, he must lean onto the prickly plants.

While walking, he hazarded a glance at the windows towering above and across the road. He spied at the family life lived matchbox-sized but with verve. Some had switched off for the day, but many lit up with late-night television, midnight snacks, and noisy games.

One of the windows on the lower floors glowed like a spiritual oasis. It was a traditional wick lamp, evident from the flickering shadows across the walls. It reminded Arun of home and his mother. He stopped to look closely at the window again.

Yes, the family had arranged everything as per tradition. An idol of Lord Krishna stood awash with the spiritual glow. A lump formed in Arun's throat. He had bought nothing to keep in front of the tiny Krishna idol in the cubby hole beside his bunk bed. No vegetables, no fruits, not even a twig of the laburnum flower that symbolised good luck and happiness. His family would be celebrating the new year back in his village.

Arun wiped away a tear. It was either sleep or hunger or nostalgia or all of it. He couldn't discern where one ended and the other began.

An approaching horn announced an oncoming train. Arun quickly pushed himself onto the hedge, getting as far away from the tracks as possible. The backpack lugged him over, and he lost his balance, causing his torso to stretch across the hedge as if crucified.

Lying on those prickly branches, cursing his sordid life, Arun's eyes fell on the loveliest sight ever. A bunch of laburnum flowers swayed above him, teasing and taunting a song of happiness from his heart. The golden shower on the tree was only a trickle, thanks to his fellow Malayalees from the neighbourhood who would have plucked away to glory. It was considered an auspicious display for Vishu.

The train passed like a noisy storm, but Arun lay enthralled, his eyes stuck on the tiny round golden petals, his mind full of images of the traditional feast, and his heart full of familial love.

THE CREDIT

The rain whistled into the shop through chinks in the roof. Mary positioned the bucket under the leakiest hole. She would usually close the shop in such a downpour, but it was six in the evening. If she closed now, what would he eat?

Mary opened her umbrella and stood outside on the narrow ledge that raised the shop by a few inches off the ground. The street was busy, and she was forced to cower under the roof jutting into the footpath. Commuters pottered around muddy puddles and skipped cautiously over rain-filled potholes.

Mary shut the umbrella and took refuge behind her burning stove. A concoction of water, milk, cardamom, and ginger simmered gently in the pan. The griddle on the other stove sat ready to singe the soft brown surface of the ladi pavs. On the corner table sat a hot box filled with spicy mashed vegetables to go with the ladi pav. The customer was the only missing piece in this picture of survival curated by the vagaries of life.

Even as her neighbours shouted at her to shut the shop doors before the wind carried away her roof, Mary waited with her eyes stuck on the street. Vimal burst into the shop like a hungry animal.

"Aunty, thank you for not closing!"

As soon as he entered, Mary shuttered the shop halfway to the ground and shoved the stool towards him. Within no time, Vimal chomped on his dinner with a cup of sweet and spiced tea. He smiled after he finished. Then, he looked around.

"How do you manage to live here, Aunty?"

Mary smiled. Vimal asked this question every day.

"You have known me for two months, yet ask me how I live here."

Vimal scratched his head with a sheepish grin.

"I know. My first two months in this city. I would have gone hungry if not for you. Tea and biscuits from Mary Aunty for breakfast, Pav Bhaji for dinner. That's my survival kit."

Mary nodded. She had taken a liking to this lad, albeit slowly. If her darling Ronnie had lived, he would have been the same age. Mary sighed as her eyes wandered up to Ronnie's framed photo on the sturdiest wall of the shop.

Vimal followed her gaze and nodded. "He'll be happy in heaven, Aunty, for sure."

Mary gathered the plate and cup from Vimal's hands and washed them in a bucket in the corner.

"Now, I have something important to tell you. I got to know of an opportunity in Dubai," Vimal said, rubbing his hands.

Mary's eyes widened. "Very good, my son."

"Before I go, I promise to pay what I owe you. One month of my breakfast and dinner charges, right?" Vimal remarked with a grin.

Mary waved her hand as if dismissing his dues.

"No, no, Aunty, I promise to pay." The rain softened a little. "I'll go now, Aunty. See you tomorrow," Vimal waved a quick goodbye and ran out of the shop.

The next evening, Mary waited with her stove burning and the griddle on low heat. Since it was not raining, she had a steady stream of customers until late at night, but the one for whom she would keep spiced tea ready did not come. He might be busy. Poor lad! He is trying his best to get a better job, she thought.

Vimal did not appear at Mary's tiny tea shop for the next three days. Then, one day, she thought she spied him across the street. She called out to him, too, but her eyes had deceived her. The young man walked briskly, oblivious to the old woman and her tea shop.

After a week, Mary opened a notebook inside a steel trunk. She ran her fingers over the photo on the first page. It was Ronnie's. Her fingers caressed his curly locks, ruddy cheeks, and broad, fair forehead. She turned the page to look at the list of names.

Mukund

Siva

Ismail

Tony

Selva

Manik

Partho

Ahmed

Babloo

Kevin

Danny

Shridhar

She took the tiny pencil inside the book and added 'Vimal' to the column. As with the others, she wrote nothing against his name. Tears streamed across her cheeks as she held the notebook to her bosom.

THE HIERARCHY OF DISCIPLINE

Som waited impatiently, his fingers tapping, knees swaying. The family poodle came for a friendly lick and was rewarded with an irritated kick.

Som wouldn't have done it at other times. At other times, he was predictable, the darling of the family, pampered, all whims and fancies catered at the hint of rage. But now, at this moment, he was a different person.

You see, Som had but one weakness. He was addicted to mangoes. And the strange world that he lived in banned mangoes and made them illegal to obtain.

Som was afraid of his father, but he also knew that if he was caught, his father would do anything to get him out of legal tangles. So, he took the risk of reaching out to the mango network. Som made friends in the network and paid them for the mangoes.

Today, he was waiting for one such friend, Santosh, a.k.a. Sandy.

Unlike Som, Sandy had no father to fear, but he yearned for his mother's happiness. He aspired for a quick change in their circumstances. A large family, several mouths to feed, and too many bills kept him awake at night. So, he found a way to make easy money.

The answer lay in the legally prohibited mangoes. Rich kids who took a fancy to the forbidden fruit would pay through their noses to get hold of it.

Sandy became the carrier. Today, he was carrying the mangoes for Som. He knew the risk. Som's father ran a tightly secured kingdom. The guards patrolled day and night. But the risks came with big rewards.

Som had a steady cash flow. Easy money also got Sandy the stuff Som had: a fancy bike and a smartphone. His siblings got what they wished for and more.

Sandy jumped over the fence, watching the guard who marched away. He dashed to the back of the house where Som had let down a rope ladder as promised. Sandy quickly shimmied up the ladder and hauled himself over the balcony wall.

"Here," he said, placing the parcel on the table.

Som pounced on them greedily.

"Wait!" said Sandy. "My money?" Som gave a wry smile and handed over the cash.

Sandy's mind boggled, but the cash was owed to many. As he pushed the wad inside his shirt, Som's father entered the balcony. One look at Sandy, and he understood why he was there. He might be a busy dad, but not totally ignorant of his son's shenanigans.

"Stop!" he shouted even as Sandy jumped over the balcony wall.

The landing was cursed. Sandy crashed to the ground with a thud and a yelp. The guards got alert, and they swarmed around him. Sandy knew that his lucky run had come to an end.

"Call the police!" one of the guards shouted.

But Som's father stopped them. "He is, after all, someone's child too. Why should we destroy his future?"

"Then what do we do with him?"

"I have a better idea. I will get him enrolled in the jungle patrol."

The guards snickered and then walked away to laugh at the joke in private. The jungle patrol was the most challenging assignment. Many did not return alive from the jungles.

"At least his family will have money and be proud of their son."

"But, Sir, the thought of the jungle patrol gives me nightmares," Sandy whimpered as he nursed his back.

"Good, it will teach you discipline."

"And what about Som, sir?"

"What about him?" the benevolent father's face darkened.

"Doesn't he need to be taught discipline?" Sandy mumbled.

"How dare you speak of my boy like that? His father is still alive to teach him."

Sandy nodded, tears rolling down his cheeks. The next day, he was packed off for his jungle patrol training. Som was found on the balcony again a few days later, waiting for his new friend from the mango network. This time it was Jugal, a.k.a. Judy.

MISAPPREHENSION

The flooded road evoked disgust. Torn plastic bags, discoloured bits of clothes, and other unidentifiable objects swirled around in the muddied waters.

Mira had to choose between wading through the yucky mess or waiting for an autorickshaw to take pity on her. She was wet, cold, and shivering despite the umbrella. It struggled against the wind to cover her and the bulky laptop bag she swung in front.

Mira cursed herself for not heeding her friends' warnings. "There is a terrible forecast for today. You better log in from home." They had cautioned.

The umbrella upturned. "Talk about throwing caution to the wind," Mira mumbled. An autorickshaw appeared in view as she corrected the umbrella. She held the umbrella in the crook of her neck, freeing her hands to wave frantically.

The driver passed by without a second look. Mira frowned. What a heartless city! She looked back at the shining glass facade behind her. If it was not for work, she would not have come here.

The autorickshaw was barely visible through the rain, but it was now coming closer instead of receding. Mira was pleasantly surprised to see the rickshaw slice through the grey water and come to a splutter beside her. The driver looked at her through bloodshot eyes. The haggard look frightened Mira. She was now hesitant to board the rickshaw but had no choice. She muttered the destination. The driver grunted in response.

Mira crouched in the backseat, hugging her bag. Her right hand was inside the front pocket, clutching her phone, ready to whip it out at a moment's notice. She had all the relevant numbers saved under emergency.

The driver was in a hurry despite the muddied water pushing back on the vehicle. As soon as they reached drier roads, he drove faster.

Mira gasped, partly due to the speed but mainly because the wind brought a nasty stink from the front. Was the driver drunk? She was about to ask him to slow down when he turned into an alley.

"Wait! Where are you going?"

"Only five minutes, madam. Please."

Mira could not understand. "What? This is not the way. Where are you going?"

"Five minutes, madam. Two minutes."

Mira perspired despite the cold weather. She whipped out her phone and called the first number on her emergency list.

The driver slowed down in front of a ramshackle house. A single bulb hung outside the front door. He ran out without a word.

Mira stopped talking mid-sentence.

"Hello? Hello?" Her roommate hollered from the other end.

Mira peered into the pouring rain. The driver had run straight into the house. From inside, she heard a wailing child and a woman trying to comfort it. The driver ran back without an umbrella or cap, dripping wet. “Sorry, madam. The baby has a fever. Medical shop near your office. We ran out of medicines.”

Mira was overcome with embarrassment and shame. “I’ll be there in ten minutes.” She messaged her roommate.

The driver got them back on route in a few minutes. When Mira refused to accept the change after paying the fare, his bloodshot eyes glistened with gratitude. She muttered a silent prayer for the baby and the family.

GLITTERING AND DARK

The bicycle paused at the fork in the road, which appeared quiet and suburban for a locality that boasted of being a microcosm of the cosmopolitan city.

Constable Morey wiped his face as he contemplated his direction. To the left was the glamorous lane with bungalows on either side. To the right was the dark alley that gave him the shudders. It led to a cemetery. Beyond the graveyard was a row of shanties huddled together for warmth. The alleyway was lit by a single working streetlight. The rest of the flickering lamps had given up on their mission long ago.

Morey looked at his new mobile, a smartphone gifted by his well-to-do brother-in-law. Should he or should he not? The day he showed his mobile to his colleagues, they asked for a treat.

"If not," said Constable Singh with a wry smile, "take a selfie in your favourite dark alley and show it to us." Singh was always envious of him. Inspector Patil joined in the fun. "I'll give you five hundred rupees, Morey, if you can do what Singh says." Patil's laugh was friendly but short.

Morey was flabbergasted. They knew how scared he was of that graveyard, and yet they teased. Can't a policeman have fears? He resolved not to fall for their trap. But his resolve shook when his only daughter asked for a fancy birthday cake. He could barely eke out the rations after sending the monthly money order to his village. How will he buy the fancy cake?

Patil's offer was still on the table. Morey could turn right and earn a few extra rupees. Instead, he turned left and cycled past the glittering bungalows. He recognised every watchman on duty at their gates. Bungalow number one, number two, number three... wait, number three was in party mode. Morey heard a loud, boisterous rendition of the Happy Birthday song.

Mili's birthday. His heart sank. He had promised Mili. A thirty-second ride through the dark alley would get him a birthday cake.

He turned around at the end of the glamour lane, back to the fork, then turned to his left and entered the dark alley without disembarking. The wheels were safer than his legs. His breath steadied as he reached the edge of the streetlight's beam. A figure moved, and Morey's feet fumbled on the pedal. The cycle shook, and he hit the ground. The figure moved closer, and Morey muttered his prayers as he closed his eyes.

"Uncle, are you ok?" said a boy, roughly ten or eleven, Morey guessed as he peeped through half-closed eyelids. The boy stood with an extended hand. Morey opened his eyes wide and scrambled to his feet. Hearing footsteps behind him, he jumped in fear.

But it was only Laxman from Bungalow number six. "Saheb, don't scold the boy. He comes here to study."

"But why sit in this dark alley? Why not the next lane? It's so bright there!"

The boy looked at Laxman. “Saheb, they don’t allow him. I mean, we don’t allow him. No trespassers.” Laxman bent his head.

The boy looked at both Morey and Laxman accusingly.

Laxman handed over a box to the boy. “My wife made something sweet today,” he said, walking away.

Morey waved the boy aside. “Sit, sit. No one will bother.”

“No one does,” the boy replied, “not even the ghosts.”

Morey remembered the bet and clicked a selfie against the backdrop of the graveyard’ wall. “Tomorrow, I’ll bring you some cake,” he said with a smile.

As Morey cycled home, he realised there were more reasons to fear the glittering lane with no trespassers than the dark alleyway with friendly ghosts.

THE ROWDY TRAIN GANG

Lissy dreaded her daily commute and the noisy ladies' compartment. Every evening, as she waited to board the local train, a rambunctious group hogged the edge of the railway platform, a position that gave them the best and the first opportunity to board the crowded local. They pushed, shoved, and nudged to the front, forcing others who were not so train-savvy to hold back.

Lissy belonged to the group that was left behind. Every day, she boarded with a fervent prayer that she would get a foothold before the train moved and enough space to squeeze into a corner. And she was happy with a corner, but the train-savvy group was not.

Once inside the train, they would continue to push, shove, yell, grimace, shout, and gesture until they made their arrogant way into the compartment. And then, they would begin their shenanigans to bag the best seats.

By the time, Lissy reached her destination and crossed over to the other entrance where her station arrived, the crowd would have dispersed, and she would hazard a condescending glance at the pushy ladies. Yes, they would have all grabbed their seats without fail.

After she disembarked, she would shake away the awful experience, straighten her spine, and resolve to never join the rowdy gang. Yes, they were rowdies. Glaring at their fellow passengers who dared to stand in front of them at the railway station, shoving the ones who blocked their way at the entrance, screaming at those who did not let them into the sitting area, and eyeing those seated as if they were thieves.

Lissy was sure that some of the ladies abandoned their seats only because of the constant threatening stares from the rowdy gang. She was getting increasingly annoyed with the group and the world in general.

Her work was nothing but monotonous. Ironically, while her mind asked for more challenges, her body yearned for less. The fifteen-minute walk to the station was becoming tiresome, and on certain days, she caught herself looking longingly at the seats inside the compartment. She swore she would buy herself a first-class pass once she got her salary increment. She deserved a quieter and more civilised commute.

If she could, she would escape from this city that never sleeps. Having arrived in Mumbai as a newlywed, she was dazzled by the speed and the energy. But the same frenetic pace now exhausted her.

The next day, she braced herself for the evening rush. Her feet were sore after the walk, and her head spun. The morning nausea spread its nagging presence until evening.

Lissy hung back at the crowd's edge, resigned to the possibility of missing the train. She can't be in the middle of the commotion in the present scenario. To her surprise, she felt an arm slip through hers and gently pull her forward. Another arm locked into hers on the other side. Before she realised it, she stood at the spot most commuters coveted.

Lissy looked around in astonishment. She was now part of the rowdy gang! The train pulled in like a pregnant woman, ready to spill out her contents at the first opportunity.

The group did their usual tricks and entered the seating area. Except, this time, and for the first time, Lissy was inside too. The first empty seat was offered to her. She sunk into it with relief and shut her eyes. When she opened them, the entire gang had taken their spots and looked at her intently.

The lady next to her offered a bottle of water.

"Thank you!" Lissy replied after she gulped down mouthfuls.

"Which month is it?" the lady sitting opposite asked.

Lissy gaped. She never imagined someone in a crowded local train would notice her barely imperceptible bump. Perhaps how her free hand held onto her tummy as she clung to the handlebar above was a giveaway. Her right hand instinctively moved to her stomach.

"Fifth."

"Still having nausea?" an elderly woman in the gang asked.

Lissy nodded.

The girl next to her sat cross-legged with a bulky book in her lap. She half-raised her eyes to look at Lissy.

"Don't worry. It'll get better," the ladies consoled in unison, except for the girl with the book. She looked up with a mild interest and continued to read.

"We noticed you've been looking tired for the past few days. You could have asked us for a seat," said the opposite woman.

"I am... was feeling fine," Lissy replied and immediately regretted the note of condescension in her voice.

The lady scoffed. "You think we're crazy. We are rowdies who grab the seats as fast as we can."

Lissy did not reply, but her lips twitched on hearing the word 'rowdies.'

The lady pointed to the elderly woman. "She is recovering from knee surgery. She doesn't have enough insurance, so she has to keep working. Jaya here has two young kids and a husband who is no better than a kid. She reaches home at ten and has scarcely enough time to cook a meal before the kids fall asleep."

Lissy turned to look at the woman she was pointing at. To her bewilderment, the woman sliced vegetables even as she smiled at Lissy. Her fingers worked so quickly that Lissy feared the lurching train would snip them off.

"Fatima is preparing for her entrance. It takes her two hours on the train, and then she goes straight to her coaching class. She gets two solid hours of study if she can sit somewhere with her heavy book."

Lissy knew who Fatima was even without looking at her. She knew the girl would not acknowledge her.

"And now you. You need the rowdy gang's help to get you safely to the other side," said the lady with a nod at Lissy's tummy.

The rowdy gang laughed in unison. A grateful Lissy joined in.

THE TRAIN FRIEND

Leena trotted beside the autorickshaw. The driver waved her away. He was not interested in small fare. She continued to jog at the same pace. A quick glance at her watch showed ten minutes to her usual train. Missing it would mean bleak chances of finding an empty seat.

Leena did not commute on the later train often enough to make friends who would block a place for her. Train friends are not found in an hour of shared suffering. The friendships are built over a lifetime of commute. A few weeks of smiles, encouraging words, and shared snacks progress into a camaraderie and kinship that matures through heartfelt exchanges.

Leena was new to the commute. She was new to the city and to the 8:12 local. In four weeks, she identified a noisy group of seven that sat together daily. Their seats were fixed, and Leena sat at the periphery two days in a row. Familiarity ensured that she got the coveted fourth seat.

The next train would not bestow such benevolence.

She slowed down her trot at the foot of the overbridge. Climb or cross? Cross, she decided in a split second as she followed a group of commuters skipping nimbly over the tracks, with heads swinging like pendulums to look out for oncoming trains. She hauled herself up to the platform with a gasp.

The commuters who had climbed the bridge were stuck on the stairs. A crowd inched forward gingerly at the entrance to the station. Leena tried to weave through the throng but was blocked by an impenetrable and jostling barricade of elbows and bags. She bid her time and focused on her toes that moved forward inch by inch. There was something wrong. The entrance was never so jampacked.

A few metres in, the crowd started splitting with audible gasps. A few women cried out loud. Leena followed a man who quickly moved away from a swooning woman. The lady was held upright by someone standing behind her.

"Paani! Paani!" Leena heard the crowd mutter as they attempted to bypass the unfit. Survival of the fittest, indeed.

A break occurred in the moving mass of industrious feet. A pair of limbs lay on the ground. Leena gasped at the sight. The soiled end of a shawl, the bag with its contents strewn over which the people hopped, skipped, and jumped.

"Don't look." An elderly voice whispered in her ear. "Accident case."

When she reached the designated position for the ladies' compartment, she knew she had missed the 8:12. The standing commute did not help allay the fear in her heart.

The following day, she was on time. She dared not cross the tracks on foot and climbed the bridge. Unlike yesterday, the platform's corners were free, and the crowd followed their usual rhythm.

Yesterday was an aberration. A blip in the morning routine. Leena found her group, but something was different. She did not have to squeeze herself into the fourth seat and had the entire third seat. She slid in, thankfully, and smiled at the lady opposite.

A sob sprang from her neighbour. She looked around at the group and realised, in horror, why she could find the empty seat. The group of seven was a group of six after the previous day's mishap. In her bid to escape tragedy, she failed to recognize a train friend lying dead on the platform.

THE DEADLY TRAIN RIDE

The man stared at his co-passengers, bemused. Not one raised their eyes, uttered a word, or moved their heads. They are all dead. The man thought, a wry smile crossing his lips.

He peeped at the one sitting next to him. The screen in his hands was as animated as the world should be, but the guy sat like a statue, eyes glued to the tiny pixels controlled by the liquid crystals.

The train stopped. The guy next to him stood up wordlessly and walked through the train door, his eyes never moving away from the screen in his hands. This could be the new structure of the human body, sooner or later, our man said aloud. No one flinched. They are all dead. The man thought with a chuckle.

He decided to play a prank. Before the train could stop at the next station, he stood up and immediately fell down in a heap. He pretended to choke, clutching his tummy and heart, making weird noises.

The passengers noticed after a few seconds. The arms moved positions, and the angles of the necks changed, but the devices remained in their hands. They looked at the man through their screens. "Someone, call the police!"

said a voice behind the screen. "Call an ambulance!" said another from behind the screen.

The man now lay motionless. The train stopped. A police patrol entered and carried the man away. "He is dead," said the passengers as they returned to their screens.

DELIVERANCE

Four pairs of eyes stared at the large brown carton by the door.

“Why did you bring it inside if you weren’t sure?” asked Asha as she eyed the box suspiciously. No one replied. Asha looked around.

Avik, beside her a few minutes ago, now moved around the room, grooving to his music.

“Avik!” yelled Asha. There was no response.

Keerthi held out a finger and slapped Avik hard on his back.

“Ow! What was that for?”

Keerthi took off his headphones and yelled into his ear. “Mom is asking you something!”

“Holy ****!” Avik moved away from Keerthi for safety and asked Asha what the matter was.

“Why did you place this box inside?” Asha repeated her question.

“What else could I do? I thought the delivery was for Keerthi.”

Asha looked at Keerthi.

“I am checking. Honestly, I don’t remember if I bought something. Let me check my pending orders,” Keerthi replied while going through her phone. “Nope, it’s not me. Dad, was it you?”

All eyes turned to Ravi, who was with them a few minutes ago, looking at the box but was now on the couch, hiding from the world behind the sheet of paper that brought worldly news. He was oblivious to any questions thrown at him.

"Dad!" yelled both Keerthi and Avik in unison.

Ravi peered over the newspaper. "Why would I order anything? I hate ordering online."

"Then do you think I would? I don't even own a credit card," Asha mumbled. "Don't just sit there. Do something. What do we do about this box?"

Keerthi nudged at Asha and pointed at Avik. He was aiming his phone at the box and saying something.

"Avik!" Asha hollered.

Avik turned around, "And this, my dear friends, is the lady of the house, tense and worried about this lonely brown box sitting in the corner of our house."

"Are you recording?" Keerthi asked. Avik gave a thumbs up. Keerthi snatched the phone from Avik's hands and deleted the video without waiting for him. "You fool, why let the world know about this? We need to be careful. We should call the police," Keerthi said as she turned to Asha.

Asha was busy on her phone.

"Mom?!"

"I am messaging my ladies' group. Maybe they have some ideas."

Keerthi rolled her eyes. “Wait. Let me call the customer service number. They would know if it’s been wrongly delivered.”

“Stupid! How will you call customer care about something you never ordered?” Avik asked with a chuckle.

Ravi finally folded up his newspaper. “I am going to open the box. It’s been addressed to me, so I should open it.”

“No!” cried three voices in unison.

Just then, Malathi came rushing through the door. “Sorry, Didi. I am late.” She rushed off inside and returned with the broom and pail the next instant. “Aah! It’s here!” she cried, running to the brown box. Before anyone could utter a word, Malathi tore open the box and took out a bulky item covered in plastic. The family stood aside, astonished.

“I asked my son to send a blanket. It’s for my mother. I’ll give it to her when we meet on Sunday,” Malathi informed. She caressed the blanket. “It’s soft.”

Asha sat down to message her friends to share the astonishing news that their maid had ordered a blanket online and sent it to their address. How incredible! Even maids are ordering online now!

Keerthi went back to ordering some more items online.

Avik asked Malathi if he could do a feature on her son, who worked for a software company. “Rags to riches stories are in great demand these days,” he added.

Ravi warned Malathi to stop using his address to get items delivered.

But Malathi was floating in the clouds. All she could think of was how quickly her son had sent her the blanket. He was a capable young man now. Her dreams had come true.

ARE WE THERE YET?

"We are more powerful than ever, but have very little idea what to do with all that power. Worse still, humans seem to be more irresponsible than ever. Self-made gods with only the laws of physics to keep us company, we are accountable to no one...

...Is there anything more dangerous than dissatisfied and irresponsible gods who don't know what they want?"

– Yuval Noah Harari

THE WRITING PARTNER

Percy tip-toed to his study without switching on a flashlight, causing him to stub his little toe against the table. Damn! The little toe and its strange attraction to furniture legs. He would have expressed his anguish aloud if not for fear of Vix.

Vix was extremely sensitive to sound and might come searching for Percy. If Vix saw him there, he would never leave. These days, he had taken a peculiar liking to Percy's study.

Percy had reached a tricky part in the tale before he went to bed the previous day. It was stuck in a strange tangle. Sleep eluded him for a couple of hours, and when he finally slipped into drowsiness, a nasty dream brought him back to anxiety. As he lay in bed, the twist magically revealed itself. He jumped out and ran into his study, and that's when he stubbed his toe.

Percy winced as he rubbed his hurt toe. Instead of pulling up the creaky chair, he picked up his notebook and pen, hobbled to the armchair, and switched on the dim portable lamp fixed on its arm.

As soon as Percy sat down, he heard a whirring. Shucks! He switched off the light. The whirring stopped. He waited for ten whole minutes before he switched on the light again.

Writing the first few lines felt like a divine intervention. The words flowed from Percy's pen like a gushing river. It took him through glades, valleys, under bridges, and near picturesque banks. He was so engrossed that he did not hear the whirring until it reached uncomfortably close.

Percy sighed and closed his pen. "Vix, how often have I told you not to enter the study when I write?"

"Yes, Percy. But yesterday, we agreed that I could be your writing partner."

"More like a sparring partner," Percy murmured. "Look, Vix. I don't need a writing partner."

Vix remained mute but did not budge. His round, blinking eyes shone like rubies, throwing dull red circles on the notebook. Percy snapped the book shut.

"Why did you stop writing? Did you need more ideas? Do you need help? Do you—"

"Vix!" Percy raised his voice. Then, he gasped as he shook his head. It wasn't Vix's fault. He was wired to help.

Percy drew a deep breath. "Ok. I got the plot twist."

"The girl on the train was a humanoid?" Vix asked.

"No... What?" Percy spluttered.

"Then, was the boy a humanoid?"

"No, why would you say that?" Percy was annoyed.

"Then the burglar was a humanoid?"

"Noooo!" Percy hollered.

"Ah, then surely the police force has a humanoid division."

"There are no humanoids in my story!" Percy shrieked. He walked off in a huff, taking his notebook and pen.

For the next few days, the story languished by his bedside. Every day, Percy would pick up the notebook, rest his pen on a blank line, sigh for a few minutes, and place the book back on the bedstand.

The only good from those soulless days was that Vix stopped badgering him. He continued to be helpful around the house but did not utter a word about being a writing partner. Percy was grateful and would have even asked Vix about his writing aspirations if not for the mail that arrived one morning. It was from AskForHelp, the company that had sent Vix to Percy's house for employment.

Thank you for encouraging your household help, Vix, to participate in the National Humanoid Writing Competition. His entry, The Burglar on the Train, won the Best Story in the Thriller category.

Please accompany him to the following address to collect his award. You are also eligible for rebates on your next monthly bill.

Percy picked up the notebook and pen to write a new story. The old one had found a new writer.

THE TEA CONTEST

The day began romantically with perfect weather, misty hills, and a tale waiting to be written. All Percy wanted to do was write a short and sweet love story in less than three thousand words. However, his misery started soon after he requested a cup of tea.

It arrived as soon as Percy made himself comfortable in his study. But while he expected a steaming hot cup of tea, there were two on his desk. And two eager teamakers stood by, staring at him intently. Percy stared back, unblinking.

Didn't they know he preferred to be left alone in the mornings?

Mary and Vix stood respectfully silent, but Percy could feel the weight of unspoken words between them.

"Well?" he raised an annoyed eyebrow.

"Please drink your tea and tell me how it is?" Mary was the first to respond. "The red cup, please."

"Percy, try mine too. It's the other one." Vix chimed in.

Percy understood what was happening. After becoming proficient in several household tasks, Vix had turned his attention to the kitchen. Mary wouldn't like it at all. As was evident from her dark eyes, boring holes into Vix's humanoid skull.

If Percy said both were good, Mary would take offence, and he would lose his cook of twenty years. If he commented

Mary's tea was better, it wouldn't help a bit because Vix would set upon the task with renewed vigour, and Percy would end up being interrupted with cups of tea until he said Vix's was better. He would never dream of saying Vix's tea was better because his life could be shortened considerably. Mary would most likely poison him in his next meal. She took her cooking quite seriously.

So, to escape the dilemma, Percy wore his writer's cloak and said, "Thanks for the tea, Mary and Vix, but I need to get in some work before I can drink it. Leave the cups of tea and me in peace for the next four hours."

Mary nodded and walked away. Vix swivelled smartly and closed the door behind him.

Percy opened his notebook in relief. He eyed both the cups. He had four hours before he gave an opinion.

The romance in the air was diminishing, and Percy was afraid that the short and sweet love story might turn into a tragedy. So, he scribbled as quickly as possible. In due course, Percy had penned around four thousand words. He leaned back in satisfaction. All it needed was some bit of editing. But his happiness melted away when he saw the two empty cups.

Percy panicked. The hour of reckoning was now upon him. He heard footsteps coming up the stairs and braced himself. It was, perhaps, a stroke of luck or a flash of genius, but his eyes fell upon Tabby, the cat curled up on the armchair.

When Mary and Vix entered the room, Percy spun a fantastic yarn. "It was not I who drank the tea. It was

Tabby, the cat!" he said, pointing an accusing finger at the feline, who looked up with practised nonchalance.

Mary looked stricken with grief while Vix added new information into his system that cats like to drink two cups of tea at once. They stomped off into the kitchen, but not before both promised to return with a cup of tea each.

Percy shooed Tabby away with a sly grin and sunk into the armchair, only to be stirred alert by the crash downstairs. There was only one way to escape the worsening situation in the kitchen. He slipped out with a Tabby-like gait into the crisp, sunny afternoon.

A GASTRONOMICAL DISCOVERY

An intense beam of light cut across the pinkish-brown sky of PT-456. Pynog sat up in his chair, anticipating an entry notification. His finger hovered over the switch. The overhead hatch required only a few seconds to open, but Pynog feared the delivery arm would drop the parcel at the wrong moment. If the package fell on the closed hatch, it would roll over the dome. A waste of precious Galactollars.

Life on PT-456 had been difficult lately, and Galactollars were hard to earn. But the pills kept him fit and satiated, and his nutritional numbers balanced. He ordered a PT-456 weeks' worth of supply every time. The delivery should arrive any time now. Pynog's health monitor beeped. He could hold out for another PT-456 day with his current hunger levels.

Alas! The light beam disappeared, and Pynog's hopes of getting his supply diminished. He spent minimal energy on his activities and waited for another day. Pynog did not have much to do besides monitoring some trash-picking activities on his screen.

The next day, a beam of light harsher than before cut across the pinkish-brown sky.

"Here it comes!" Pynog murmured and pressed the switch at the exact moment. The delivery arm reached through the hatch and gently dropped the package on the table below.

Pynog tore open the package in a hurry. He was on the brink of starvation. Out fell a note that apologised for the delay.

"We faced traffic congestion as the Intergalactic Highway Maintenance Department cleared space debris. Sorry for the delay. We offer you a discount of twenty Galactollars on your next purchase."

Inside the package was a box. Pills were never delivered in boxes. Pynog opened the box and inhaled the strangest of smells. The aroma that hit his nostrils was so strong that he kept the box aside to take deep breaths of the PT-456 air.

"What kind of a joke is this!?" Pynog yelled. "I want a refund!" He punched in the code to talk to a Galaxxiggy representative. "What have you sent me?" He held up the opened box for the representative to see.

"I am sorry, Sir, but it looks fresh."

"Fresh! Freshhh!" Pynog screamed. "I don't care about fresh. Tell me what this is!"

The representative held up his hands. "It's a heritage food called chilli chicken."

Pynog stared at the representative with a face contorted into a combination of befuddlement, astonishment, and disgust. One of his eyebrows twitched on its own accord.

"Isn't that the avian species that went extinct centuries ago?"

"Err, well, yes."

Pynog dropped the box onto the table in disgust. "What is this made of then? Its carcass or its paleontological remains buried under the rocks?"

"Neither, sir. They make the protein in the laboratory. They are making it the good old way."

Pynog shook his head. "Such ancient technology still exists!"

"It's heritage food, Sir, like I said."

"But who orders them these days?"

Just then, another person joined them on screen.

"Hello, Sir," said the Galaxxiggy representative. He spoke to the other person. "I am sorry, Sir, your delivery got mixed up with this customer from PT-456."

The other customer groaned. "Switching orders will take ages with the debris cleaning programme."

Pynog, now curious, asked, "Where are you located, if I may ask?"

"PT-789."

Pynog nodded. "You are right. No point switching now." He inhaled the smell from the box again. "It seems ok. I might just eat this. But you must deliver my order as soon as possible, free of cost."

"We agree to do so, Sir." The Galaxxiggy representative turned to the customer from PT-789. "Sir, will you consume the order you received or…?"

"I was craving some heritage food," he said, staring at the unappetising pills in the package he received. "But I might just keep these as a backup for hungry days. That doesn't absolve Galaxxiggy, though. I deserve a free delivery, too."

The Galaxxiggy representative sighed. He was going to lose Galactollars from his salary.

Pynog took a bite of the chilli chicken, and his mouth exploded with flavour. His eyes widened, and his tongue craved more. The customer from PT-789 watched him with a sly smile. Pynog's eyes expressed gratitude even as the screen switched off.

FREEDOM MIRAGE

The alarm beeped in an increasing crescendo. Shamik gasped as he caught his breath on the run. Running in the heat was a bad idea, but he had no choice. He was running short of essentials and had to reach the nearest medical kiosk as quickly as possible. Shamik chose his pitstops carefully. Break before noon and walk after five in the evening. Sleep in between.

Despite all the planning, he lost his way. He stopped to survey the land. Vast stretches of sand and rubble gleamed in the morning sun. Shamik searched his pockets without even bothering to wipe his dripping face. Not a single capsule remained. He cursed himself.

Shamik had been the top project manager at his organization, driving every critical mission to success. But within six months of having entered the Free Riders Network, he seemed to have lost the ability to plan. As a last resort, Shamik took out his phone and called the FRN emergency service. It cost him expensive communication minutes.

"Hello? The nearest medical kiosk, please."

An automated voice said, "Coordinates sent, Sir."

Shamik clutched the beacon of hope in his palm. It was the only luxury he allowed himself when he scaled down his lifestyle.

Six months ago, he was one of the fifteen thousand humans retrenched by his company. They offered him two options. He could live inside Optimum City on a premium lifestyle package, enjoying all the benefits enjoyed by the top one percent of the human population, or live outside the city in the wild on a subsidized package from the Free Riders Network. The subsidized pack had essential benefits, including the subsistence capsules to be taken once daily to survive.

Inside Optimum City, the citizens could live under optimal climactic conditions and savour the choicest foods, but they were all monitored physically, mentally, emotionally, and physiologically. Every Optimum citizen automatically signed up for the Ideal Human Research Programme, whose mission was to make humans the best possible versions of themselves in all respects. They could not leave the city unless they were thrown out.

Shamik harboured dreams of travelling even as a child. He chose to exit Optimum City and live in a run-down hostel on the outskirts. And now he was suffering, running low on his subsistence capsules ten days into his exploratory trip.

The planned pitstop for food supplies was not due until tomorrow. He surveyed the land again and saw the blue flag denoting the presence of a medical centre.

Shamik half ran, half stumbled to the building, rushed towards a kiosk in the corner, and slammed his hand on the button to get a packet of capsules. Enough to survive two more weeks. By then, he would be at his next planned pitstop.

After he swallowed his pill, he felt his pulse become normal. The alarm from his watch had stopped beeping long back, giving up on its foolish owner, who forsook his chance to be inside the great Optimum City.

"Welcome to Optimum City," said an attractive lady on the screen above the kiosk. A video showcased all the benefits and amenities that the citizens of Optimum City enjoyed. Shamik stood mesmerized, although he had seen the video before. The serenading music and the alluring scenes captured his attention completely. Before he knew it, he was walking towards a door on the other side of the medical centre. He strolled as if in a daze. An entrance to Optimum City was straight ahead. A yawning hole appeared in the wall as he reached the dome-shaped structure. A lady with the sweetest smile stepped out. She was followed by a team of security personnel. They all looked eager to welcome him into their fold.

Shamik walked up to them in a trance. He smiled at the lady and security team, nodded his thanks, and stopped abruptly. It was only now that he noticed. The lady and all the other men and women in the security team resembled each other like they were clones. All of them looked alike.

Shamik shuddered and trembled as he heard them speak in unison, "WELCOME TO OPTIMUM CITY!"

He turned and ran straight through the medical centre and into the arid desert.

"Better to be free than conform!" He yelled as he disappeared into the mirage of freedom.

A BETTER PLACE

The instructions mentioned a colossal banyan tree with a wooden bench under it. I had to take a right turn from the landmark. Someone had helpfully added the new milestone in brackets (a charging station with a kiosk). I wondered if the remnants of the missing tree would break through the kiosk someday.

Next came the house with a mango tree peeping over its garden wall, (in brackets, Grand Shopping Mall). I sighed in relief. That's an easier landmark to identify compared to a mango tree. I tried hard to recall what a mango tree looked like. I wouldn't have recognized it even if it had survived.

I walked along unhurriedly since I didn't want to raise any suspicions. The Special Intelligence Unit had cameras everywhere, and they monitored everyone. Anyone found acting strange could be hauled up for questioning. I had suffered it once when I was quietly reading a book about trees sitting on my balcony.

The cops came out of nowhere and whisked me off in their limousine. I had never ridden a limo before and was enamoured by the interiors, but my excitement soured when they asked me ridiculous questions. Are you a rebel? Why are you reading about trees? Do you plan to grow something in your garden? Do you know planting anything other than ornamental plants is against our policy? Have you taken your nutrition pills today? And so on.

I had to take a test to convince them that I knew nothing about fruits and vegetables or even animal protein. Little did they know I could game the quiz to look like a nature denier. They dropped me off at my front gate without confiscating my book. And that was their mistake.

The book was magic. Hidden among its pages were instructions on how to reach the Magical Forest. I had picked up this well-thumbed copy from a garbage bin. Someone had made valuable additions to the instructions, like the next one.

Pass by the banana orchard with a pond beside it (in brackets, Panda Nutritional Laboratory). A succinct modern replacement for the orchard. I gaped at the shiny new facade of the monstrous building. Employees—humans and others— buzzed in and out of the gate.

Walking further, I noticed the cameras were few and far between. Taking care to not stare at them for long, I counted the number of steps. Fifty to the first one. Hundred to the next. Hundred and twenty to the third. I kept counting until I came to the seventh.

Congratulations! There are no more cameras after this.

Whoever wrote the additional notes had made meticulous observations for the followers' benefit.

I reached the outskirts of my city. A line of shrubbery began by the road almost as abruptly as the spy poles with mounted cameras ended. Approximately a hundred steps away was a break in the shrubbery. I turned into the path and caught my breath. This was it. The way to the Magical Forest.

The shrubbery gave way to taller plants, trees, and even taller trees. I gasped as my eyes roamed all over the green dome above me. I hadn't seen so many trees together in my life. Strolling straight into the forest, I found what I was looking for. My favourite guavas. I plucked a ripe one from the tree and inhaled its sweet fragrance. I remembered how my mother would add salt and red chilli powder to sweet, ripe guava slices on a hot summer afternoon. It was bliss.

I took out the salt and chilli powder tins hidden in my pockets and the Swiss knife, all heirlooms from my mother's kitchen. I could be arrested if someone from the SIU considered raiding my house.

I savoured the first slice but swallowed the rest quickly. The tiniest sound from the forest sent shudders down my spine. What if someone had followed me?

I looked at another one. It was tempting. But I shook the craving off. The instructions were clear. Take only one fruit at a time. Gosh! How will I make another trip to relish another one? I didn't believe I had the nerve to do it again. Unless!

I read through the last line. If you want to enjoy more, take one of the saplings from the forest and plant it in your garden. I looked around and found the innocent plant babies in neatly arranged pots. I could be arrested for non-compliance and could spend the rest of my life in a highly sanitized, deaddiction and recovery centre where they would cure me of any unwanted cravings for food. But I took one anyway, and instead of returning to that blasted city, I walked along the road lined with shrubs.

There had to be a better place.

SUPER BABY

A flat grey device flew across the hall and landed on the marble floor with a crack. "There is nothing in this contract that holds them liable!" T yelled. An arm monitor beeped ominously, making him wince. He rummaged through his ornate desk. "Where is it, you fool?" T yelled again.

The desk spoke in a staccato voice. "Please name the item you are looking for, Sir?"

"My afternoon shot!" T's voice shrieked across the hall to the opposite end, where P meditated.

The drawer opened from the left end of the desk and raised itself to T's height. He took the pill and calmed down immediately.

P seemed to have taken hers already because she was entirely at peace despite the racket he created.

He strolled across the hall. "How are you so calm?"

P looked up and smiled beatifically. "It's a new course I am doing. Helps me forget my surroundings."

T sighed and sank into a cushioned sofa nearby. "Nothing in the contract says we can sue them if our child runs away."

P smiled again, but the curve of her lips portrayed scorn. "You are rich enough to own the company and still considering suing them?"

T closed his eyes and relaxed on the sofa. "I don't see a need to own SuperBabies, as long as I can track down my own super baby."

P threw her hands in the air and conjured up a screen. "Look."

T opened his eyes wearily.

The world's fastest criminal steals trillions of dollars said the headlines. The article went on about the criminal mastermind who breaks the most complicated computer codes and then, just for fun, breaks into government offices, steals files, and runs away at lightning speed.

"I asked them for the fastest and strongest baby so he could be an athlete," T muttered slowly.

"And I asked for the most intelligent baby. We got what we asked for. How can we sue them?" P replied.

"How can you be sure that's him? He ran away from home. He has left no digital trace, and—"

"Because the world's best brains have been unable to catch him. I know it's him," P replied with a certainty that scared T.

P walked over to the balcony.

"Besides, didn't we teach him that money is the most important thing in this world?" she asked as she stared out from the forty-fourth floor of their mansion at the sparkling city they owned.

SHERU AND DOLBY

The plane scraped the runway like a drunkard dragging his feet on the tarmac. Andy was the last to leave his seat and collect his luggage. The task assigned to him left him listless.

When Grandma passed away, everyone except him made it to the ancestral house. He was out on an expedition to Antarctica. As a climate scientist, his job took him to the most inhospitable regions of the globe, and they were growing in number.

Next year, his team would visit India to study the coastline. He asked his family if he could complete his task then. But that would mean a delay of five months. No one wanted to pay for Dolby's services for that long. The family believed Andy, a scientist, was the best person to handle Dolby. He had neither the time nor inclination to explain that Dolby was not his area of expertise.

On his way home from the airport, he read through the FAQs on the AIPets Inc. website. The process was straightforward. Why did they need a scientist for this?

Grandma's neighbour offered his condolences while handing the keys to the house. Andy opened the front door and went straight to Grandma's room. All her belongings lay intact. Dolby was secure inside his cabin. He looked eerily preternatural without any juice left in him, like a stuffed animal.

Andy spent the night at the house as his appointment with AIPets was scheduled for the next day. After a simple dinner offered by the neighbours, Andy fluffed up his pillow in his old bedroom. No sooner had his head touched the pillow than a low moan arose outside the window. Andy shot up like an arrow. The crying continued for nearly a minute. It changed to a whine and reached a crescendo. He opened the window and peered into the darkness below.

Andy discerned a canine form in the dim light of the lamp outside grandmother's bedroom window. It was Sheru. No photos of Grandma were ever complete without her favourite mutt. The family disapproved of him, a rescue dog, and persuaded her to send him away when Dolby arrived. But somehow, he would always turn up at their doorstep.

Sheru looked up as Andy called out his name. The brown tail wagged meekly. Andy went down to the front door and called out again. Sheru came around, panting, dragging his four legs and a tired tail. Andy went inside to dig through his knapsack. There was a packet of biscuits. But the offered food was rejected. He didn't know what to do with this mourning dog. He sat fondling his floppy ears until day broke, and it was time for his bus to the city.

When he was ready to leave, Andy ruffled Sheru's hair and left the biscuits in a bowl at the door. The neighbour had offered a lift to the bus stop. As Andy carried Dolby's case to the neighbour's car, Sheru gave him a doleful look. "Can't take you with me, buddy," Andy whispered.

At AIPets Inc., they gave a long form with questions about security, privacy, permission to use the data, and any videos recorded by Dolby when he guided Grandma. Every bit of data inside Dolby's system belonged to Andy's family, but the company invariably hoped to get access to it for research purposes.

Andy revoked all permissions. Dolby would be reset, his data wiped clean, ready for a new patron looking for an intelligent pet that worked on battery. A low-maintenance dog that required no petting, walking, or feeding. A yearly contract for maintenance and a ten-year warranty would ensure Dolby's health. As they removed Dolby from his case and checked for any physical damages, Andy wondered if he would remain a Dolby with his next family as well? The name was Andy's suggestion to Grandma, referring to their shared love for music.

"The new family will choose one for him. He'll be as good as new. Nothing of his current life would remain with him," the company representative assured Andy.

A few days later, as Andy prepared for his next expedition, he paused while he read a message from Grandma's neighbour. Sheru had died at their doorstep. The neighbour had done what was required. "He simply stopped eating. I think he missed her."

Andy wished he had known how to wipe away Sheru's memories like they did to Dolby.

RINGO FLIES AWAY

Ringo flew over the treetops in circles. He kept an eye on every branch, hovering like a kestrel. Ringo's job was simple -- to look out for invasive species of birds and eliminate them as soon as spotted.

Not one bird had pierced through the park's defences in the last three months. Ringo's training was highly specialized and perfect. After months of research and gruelling sessions, the Parks Protection Board developed the BIRDCATCHER's training module. The rising imbalance in the species created an emergency, and the Board came under pressure for a while, but they put the best brains available to the task. Ringo was one of their early releases. He had soared high into the sky amidst a cheering, clapping crowd that gathered at the park.

Ringo flew to the eastern corner first, then cut across to the west, swerving to the north, and finally ending with the southern end. The pattern for his flight was the same every day. Until one day, he changed it.

Ringo flew east as usual, but instead of flying back to the western corner, he turned to the north and hovered above the dense treetops in circles. His sharp telescopic eyes spotted a suspicious flying movement. The usual protocol would be to fly nearer to the target, switch on the laser fitted on his claws, and shoot. But this time, he delayed it.

The movement was that of a species known to be highly invasive, but it was not just one bird. It was a nest full of chicks, with their mouths open, ready to be fed by the mother bird flitting nearby.

The camera in Ringo's telescopic eyes activated automatically, and a report reached the Park Board headquarters that a nest had been missed during the daily surveillance. A massive error in Ringo's functioning.

The supervisors noted that Ringo had not yet activated the laser. "What is he doing?" they asked one another.

Ringo moved closer to the target but showed no predatory actions. He observed the tiny chicks for a while, cocking his head this way and that way.

"What's wrong with him? He is supposed to take immediate action! Call the Robotics division!"

The Robotics division, meanwhile, was already making amends. 'BIRDCATCHER GONE ROGUE. IMMEDIATE deployment of Shazam to Northwood Park,' the robotics division relayed to the Parks Board.

Ringo sensed another predator in the vicinity. Shazam burst into the skies above the nest with glowing flappers and shining red eyes. Ringo took aim instantly. The flappers glowed for one final time, and the eyes shone like red embers as Shazam dropped to the ground in a heap of electronic debris.

Ringo flew across the northern sky and outside the park borders. His mechanical flappers took flight to freedom like actual wings.

EERIE TALES

"Monsters are real, and ghosts are real too. They live inside us, and sometimes, they win."

– Stephen King

A CLEAN APARTMENT

Riya gulped in a mouthful of air as she stepped out of Heathrow airport. It was the first time, and her heart thumped in excitement. But her breath clung to her throat, making her cough out the dampness.

An airport staff walked up to her. "Are you waiting for the black cab?"

Riya could have sung her words in reply. She was happy that someone other than an immigration officer or a security personnel spoke to her. The friendly tone added to the happiness. Until now, the few who talked to her appeared dubious of her intentions. They stared as if she should not exist in this world. She used the politest expressions to convey that she was in their country only on a work project, not to establish dominion. Finally, they let her go with an air of awarding a lottery.

After such demoralizing encounters, Riya felt grateful for the man's innocuous question. But still, her tongue had gone thick on her.

The man raised a quizzical brow. Riya swallowed her dry diffidence. She nodded in acknowledgment instead of trying to get her tongue unstuck.

A black cab rolled up just then, and she set out to an unknown location in an unfamiliar country. The cab driver appeared a bit morose, and Riya was glad. She only wished to take in the sights. Conversations were not necessary. The wide roads bordered with green gradually gave way to crowded city lanes.

Within an hour, Riya stood on the pavement by a nondescript door. She rummaged in her pocket for the instructions. The service apartment providers had sent her a detailed mail before leaving for London. Riya entered the passcode at the door, which unlocked with a click. However, after the swift click, the door was slow to budge. Riya tussled with it until she could get her bags and suitcase inside.

The door promptly clicked behind her while she looked for the lockbox in the empty lobby. It was a sham of an entryway. Riya and her bags took half of the elongated space beneath the stairs. If someone were to push open the main door at that moment, they would have to use their might against the solidly muscular and hefty bags packed by an Indian family for their beloved daughter.

Riya keyed in the passcode in the lockbox and inserted her hand into the sacred space. A bunch of keys and an envelope lay inside. The whole act reminded her of treasure hunts and game shows. Clutching the contents of the lockbox, she hauled up the first set of bags to the second floor, where she found another door. Only one flat on every floor. Riya shook her head.

A lonely building.

She worried about the unchaperoned suitcase in the lobby below as she pushed open the door to place her bags. But they were safe unless the thief and the luggage were as silent as cats while they escaped the lobby.

The building was eerily silent.

Inside the room, Riya switched on the television for company. The envelope contained another set of instructions for the serviced apartment. The television, the DVD player, the Wi-Fi connection, the dishwasher, the washing machine, the heater— Riya mentally ticked off all the amenities listed as she went through the tiny living room, kitchen, and the smaller bedroom. The apartment was designed to offer Riya a comfortable night's sleep after she slogged at the workplace. There was even a glass desk at one end of the living room with a street view.

The street below was a sharp contrast to the apartment. It hustled and bustled with life. And to her surprise, the large facade across the street announced it was a market. Riya perked up at the thought of a quaint little market in central London. It would make her evenings after work more bearable.

At work, Riya made friends as quickly as she dispensed smiles. They pulled her into their circles and introduced her to the eateries around. She enjoyed eating out but preferred to cook at home.

Riya invited some friends for dinner one day, and they appreciated how spic and span everything looked.

"You are a neat housekeeper!"

"How do you have the energy after work?"

"This place looks fabulous!"

Riya beamed with pride. It was a first for her. To have her own space and then have guests appreciate her housekeeping skills. She was not known for such talents back home. Her eyes lit up when her guests enjoyed the curry she had prepared.

"I am getting bored of outside food. I might start bringing lunch from home," she said casually. Her colleagues nodded in appreciation. The dinner was a success, although Riya noticed the glances exchanged among the four while their restless eyes roamed the apartment.

One of her friends asked for the bathroom. As Riya showed her to the bedroom, she sensed a hesitation. Before closing the bathroom door, her colleague called her, "Stay here in the room, will you?"

Riya was puzzled by the girl's request. Her colleague stepped out, sauntered to the window, and peered into the quadrangle below. Conversations punctuated with laughter and shrieks wafted through the windows of the building across the quadrangle.

The girl remarked, "What ruckus!"

"They have many friends coming over, I suppose," Riya said with a shrug.

"It seems quiet in here, though," said her colleague.

"Yes, it's peaceful once I close the windows and draw up my curtains."

"Would be nice to sleep in here, right?"

Riya nodded in agreement, but a flicker of doubt passed across her eyes. "The street outside is quite noisy over the weekend," Riya added. "Many tourist groups roaming around. I think there are guided tours as well."

“But it’s quiet in here?” her colleague persisted.

“Yes?” Riya was on edge.

After they left, Riya threw the leftovers into the trash bag, tied it up, and stuffed it deeper into the trash can. As she lay in bed, she went through the bizarre questioning by her colleague. The room was indeed quiet and comfortable. It was so silent that she could easily immerse herself in her meditative playlist. Within no time, Riya drifted off to sleep.

The next day, she got up fresh and full of lunch ideas. She had to wake up thirty minutes earlier than usual to make lunch, but she did not mind. Once she packed, she pushed the leftovers into the fridge. It would be a good accompaniment for bread in the evening.

But, when she returned from work, the curry had vanished from the refrigerator! Moreover, the kitchen was tidied, the sink cleaned, plates and glasses dried, and the trash can was emptied!

Riya sat on her couch, her palms sweating, her forehead producing beads of perspiration. And then she stuck her palm to her forehead. This was a serviced apartment! The management had sent someone to clean it. She chuckled at her unnecessary panic. That was an excellent joke to pass around at the lunch table.

Her colleagues teased her about forgetting that it was a serviced apartment.

“Yes, but for nearly three weeks, I did the cleaning as well!”

“And all the time, we thought you had exceptional cleaning skills!” her colleague guffawed.

"Imagine! I felt so proud." Riya shook with laughter.

Gradually, it became a routine because Riya had seen her mother pack off the leftovers at home for their maid. So, she kept some food in the fridge every day, which would disappear by evening. Someday, Riya hoped to see the one who cleaned her apartment while she was away. She wondered if she should ask the management, but work kept her busy, and she forgot all about it.

The project was a huge success. Riya had a celebratory party with her colleagues.

"Have you seen your mystery cleaner yet?" asked one of her colleagues.

"No, which is sad because the work was so good. I wished to give a parting gift to the person."

"But you have been feeding them some good Indian food every day. I think that should have kept them happy."

"Still, do you think I could leave some cash before I go?"

"No, you shouldn't. I am sure it would be against the management policy," one of her colleagues commented. Others nodded in agreement.

Riya sighed.

It felt wrong to leave the place without meeting the person. After much deliberation, before leaving for the airport, she wrote to the management, asking them if she could get the address of the person who had cleaned her apartment. She would like to thank them personally since they had done such a good job.

The reply came a day later.

Dear Ms. Riya,

We are glad that you liked the work done by our cleaning staff. We shall convey your gratitude on your behalf.

However, it is against our company policy to divulge the personal details of our staff.

We also apologize for the lack of cleaning services during the final two weeks of your stay at our serviced apartment. The cleaning staff fell ill, and we couldn't find a replacement.

We have processed a discount on your service fees. It will be transferred to the company accounts in a few days. We sincerely hope that you were not inconvenienced.

We hope to serve you in the future.

Thank you,

Ford Service Apartments

Riya read the email twice, then read it thrice after ten minutes. She read the reply twenty times that day until she was afraid to look at it. She checked the sender's email. She verified her own email address. She confirmed the office address in the signature. All the details matched the location where she stayed.

But how could it be?

The vanishing food, the emptied trash can, the clean kitchen, and the tidied rooms?

Riya opened the chat to look for one of her colleagues in London.

Hi!

Hiya! How are you, Riya? Hope you reached home safe and sound.

Yes! Thanks!

We missed your lunchbox yesterday. Ha-ha!

Hey! I need to ask you something.

Ok? Shoot.

I rec'd a weird mail from the mgmt. of the apt… where I stayed.

The reply came after a few seconds. Riya sensed the hesitation.

Did you, now?

Yes. I'll forward it to you.

Copy Saba as well.

Saba?

Yes, Saba.

Saba was the girl who kept asking her how quiet the bedroom was. Riya forwarded the mail. Saba appeared on chat almost magically.

You got it, too, didn't you? Gosh! I wasn't crazy after all! No one believed me!

What do you mean, Saba?

I had a similar experience while staying at that place!!!

Why didn't you tell me?!

Well, I kept asking you if the apartment was quiet at night?!!!

And it was.

It wasn't when I stayed there! I would hear weird sounds.

What sounds?

Someone moaning, whining, crying, sobbing at intervals.

WTF?!

But you didn't hear?!

No!

And then Riya realised she would always switch on her playlist when she went to sleep.

I would plug in my earphones. At night. I listen to music before sleeping.

And you keep the volume loud?!

Yes. Usually. It's a habit I picked up in my teens. It drowns out any loud noises. Mumbai is a noisy city.

Talking about the city! Google for the history of the street where you stayed.

Why?

Just google. I am not sure, but you never know.

Saba had seemed strange when she visited Riya at her apartment. Now, she sounded mysterious.

Riya searched for the place. Her eyes widened as she read. The location was infamous as the site for gruesome serial murders of women. Jack the Ripper had ensured that the place was now a popular tourist spot. Guided tours took the visitors on terror walks.

Riya wondered if nineteenth-century ghosts liked spicy Indian food.

THE CRIME

Ghissu checked the camera angle one last time. He couldn't ignore it any longer. He had to catch the thief red-handed.

Four packets of chips on four consecutive nights.

Although he agreed to his nephew's suggestion of placing a camera in the store, he didn't trust it completely. Ghissu decided to keep watch along with the camera. Whoever sneaked in must open the noisy shutter first.

He placed a chair behind the counter and waited. Soon, he began dreaming of the new department store he would open. Two, three, or four times as large as his small convenience shop on the village outskirts. He would move to the city, away from the poverty, the jungle, away from...

What was that?! Ghissu returned from dreamland with a jolt. There was a scraping sound from one of the shelves at the back. He jumped up to investigate. The shutter was still down, but the store was bathed in a dull light seeping through the chinks in the windows.

Ghissu pointed his flashlight towards the shelf and stepped forward on light feet. The flashlight threw rings of light on the fully stocked shelves. Nothing moved. He lifted his bare foot ahead and stepped on a crunchy object.

A packet of chips.

His eyes lit up with smug authority and then squinted in puzzlement. He seemed to have prevented a theft, but who entered and how?

He examined the packet, which triggered a Deja vu.

Ghissu recognized the bloodied fingerprints on the package. He fainted with a barely audible scream.

****

A week ago, a boy with tousled hair and a grimy face entered Ghissu's store. He looked thin but not frail. His eyes shone as they wandered around.

Recognizing the boy as a forest dweller, Ghissu asked gruffly, "What do you want?" The boy shrugged. Ghissu's suspicious eyes followed the boy as he wandered to the back. He found it repulsive that the boy and his people couldn't afford to buy anything but would enter the store to gawk. The boy stopped by a shelf.

Ghissu's eyes strained to catch the boy's action, but his attention was diverted by the entrance of a group of stout, muscular men. They came in yelling for cigarettes. They frequented the store on the way to the forest. He suspected that they liked to hunt. He could swear that he had seen a gun inside their jeep. Such men should not be trifled with, so he smiled a lot, bowed obsequiously, and praised their health.

As one of the men lit his cigarette, Ghissu noticed the boy sneaking away with a packet of chips.

"Stop! Thief!" he shouted.

The boy ran. The men scampered after him. Ghissu couldn't leave his store unattended, so he waited outside. The boy sped into the jungle with the men in hot pursuit.

Ghissu couldn't take his eyes off the thicket where they disappeared but was forced to go inside when a customer arrived. Time and money wait for no man.

In the evening, one of the men returned with the packet of chips. "You don't worry about anything. We are here to protect," he said with a sneer.

Ghissu bowed, smiled, and praised, but his words got stuck in his throat when he saw the packet. The man left before he could ask about the blood stains. He threw the packet away in disgust.

****

When Ghissu woke up, he was still lying on the floor where he had fainted the previous night. The packet of chips remained where he had dropped them. His nephew yelled and banged on the store shutter. Ghissu quickly threw the pack into the waste basket and opened the shutter. "What happened? Why so late? How was the watch?" The nephew quizzed.

Ghissu did not answer.

The nephew fiddled with the camera. "Let's see if it worked. I don't know if they swindled us with an old camera." He played the night's visuals, nodding gleefully at the clarity until, at one point, he froze. His eyes fixed on his uncle in a terrified stare.

Ghissu walked across to check out the video.

A packet of chips flew from the shelf, floated like a fairy in the air, and then fell down when Ghissu switched on the flashlight. No one was visible, and no hand carried it.

Ghissu fainted again.

ERROR 404, NOT FOUND

"Unit number 404."

The guard pretended to not hear it right. "What did you say?"

The delivery man chuckled. "I know, right? Error. Not found," he said, punctuating his wisecrack with an alarming croak.

The guard looked even more astonished. "What?"

The delivery guy sobered up. "404." He yelled.

The guard muttered under his breath. He checked the address on the parcel cover. It was indeed 404. The delivery man was right. Shaking his head, the guard pushed the register toward the man, who signed his name— Andy.

Andy whistled a tune as he reached the elevator. Dialling the unit number sent him into another paroxysm of chuckles. He will have a whale of a time in the evening narrating this to his colleagues in the coding class. Andy's chuckling stopped when he received no response from the unit. He dialled again. No response. He could update the delivery status as undelivered and return, but he would have to return to attempt another delivery. A waste of time. So, he tried again.

This time, a sweet female voice replied. "Hello?"

"Deliveryyyy!" Andy yelled through the phone.

"Come in," the voice replied, sounding faint.

At the door to unit number 404, Andy rang the bell. Again, there was no response.

The folks at 404 appeared to be a lazy lot. He rang thrice until the door opened. But to his surprise, there was no one at the door. Should he leave the parcel on the doorstep?

A faint whisper caught his ears. Error. Not Found. Error. Not Found. Error. Not Found...

Andy stepped in through the door, mesmerised. He entered an empty living room, and the door closed behind him.

A few days later, the guard looked astonished for the second time in a week. A parcel for unit number 404 again. Who was ordering these things? Wasn't it empty? He asked his colleague who was lost in his phone and didn't respond.

The new delivery guy signed his name— Selva.

Selva did not find anything odd about the unit number, nor was he in on Andy's joke. He had known Andy only for a few weeks and had met him once or twice at the delivery pick-up location. But Andy seemed to be missing lately. He probably found another job. In the gig economy, few colleagues kept track of each other. All Selva knew was that Andy's route was now his responsibility.

Selva dialled the unit number and waited. No response. He would dial once more and leave a 'We missed you' ticket inside the letterbox at the entrance. After dialling the second time, he was about to turn away to look for the letterbox when he heard a faint voice. A male voice spoke, "Hello?"

"Delivery?" Selva intoned.

"Come in," the voice replied.

At the door to unit 404, Selva waited after ringing the bell thrice. Gosh! He had many other deliveries for the day. Just when he placed the parcel on the doorstep, the door opened. "Your delivery—" Selva was interrupted by a faint murmur inside the apartment.

Error. Not Found. Error. Not Found. Error. Not Found...

Selva stepped in, mesmerised. As he reached the empty living room, the door closed behind him...

NOURISHING TALES

"Food, it appeared, could be important. It could be an event. It had secrets."

– Anthony Bourdain

THE CLAY POT

"Crash!"

Shobha ran to her kitchen balcony, fearing the worst. She peered through the recesses. Her reddish-brown pot lay in smithereens six floors below. This would create a furore in the residents' group. Hazardous objects falling from the sky.

"Psst!" A hiss from the opposite balcony.

Shobha folded her hands. "I'm sorry. I don't know how it fell," she mouthed.

Auntie Lin waved away her apology. Shobha grinned.

Shobha met Auntie Lin the day they arrived in the country six months ago. A sturdy middle-aged woman with greying hair greeted her as she entered the elevator. Auntie Lin helped her adjust to the new environment. The condominium was smaller than Shobha's ancestral home, yet the household chores overwhelmed her. "Ah! Newlyweds! Can enjoy, lah!" Auntie Lin would cheer with a wink. An avid cook, Shobha created a familiar world inside an unfamiliar city with her food. Her favourite was always the fish curry. It was best prepared in her mom's earthen pot, the remnants of which were swept away by the cleaners this morning.

Her doorbell rang. It was Auntie Lin. "How will you make fish curry now?"

"I don't know."

"Wait!" Auntie Lin rushed into her house and returned with a big black wok.

"It's too big."

"You make more and share," Auntie Lin said with a wide grin.

"Not going to the fish market until Friday."

Auntie Lin nodded in disappointment.

The next day, she knocked on Shobha's door with a blue plastic bag. A fishy smell hit Shobha's nostrils. She accepted wearily. Her original dinner plans did not include fish curry.

The evening passed, but no fish curry went to the neighbour's house.

Auntie Lin rang Shobha's doorbell the following day. "You tried?"

"I did, but I ran out of tamarind. I used tomatoes instead. It didn't taste the same."

"Ah! Tamarind is easy to get." And off went Auntie Lin before Shobha could tell her it was not the usual tamarind. Shobha messaged her that it was called the Malabar Tamarind. She replied with a thumbs up.

Auntie Lin returned soon, beaming from ear to ear. "I asked a friend. She got it for me. Now try."

Shobha nearly shut the door in Auntie Lin's face. Her persistence bordered on neurosis.

No fish curry passed the threshold that evening.

Her husband eyed the reheated fish curry. “There’s so much left. Why don’t you give some to Auntie Lin? She loves your fish curry.”

“It hasn’t turned out well.”

“Didn’t she get you the fish?”

“And the wok,” Shobha muttered.

The next day, Shobha visited Auntie Lin. Her beaming smile fell when she noticed the wok in Shobha’s hands.

“Auntie Lin, the curry is tasty only if cooked in an earthen pot.”

“I can ask my friend, who—”

“Any new pot has to be cured. I don’t know how to do it.”

The following day, when Shobha heard the doorbell, she wondered what Auntie Lin could be up to next.

“I got this for you,” Auntie Lin said, proudly holding a clay pot. “Same as earthen, no?”

Shobha considered the clay pot. The base was thick and heavy. It had a single round handle, making it look like a large-headed spoon.

“I can try.”

Auntie Lin clapped her hands in glee.

Shobha’s husband got the fish, but no curry passed the threshold for the third consecutive day.

“Today’s fish curry was fantastic!” he remarked.

“It’s not good enough. I need our earthen pot.”

"So, you didn't share the curry with Auntie Lin today?"

"No. If a curry goes out of this house, it has to be perfect, or it doesn't pass this threshold. You are not a connoisseur, but Auntie Lin is. She'll discern the lack of flavour."

Shobha and Subhash spent the weekend exploring the city. Auntie Lin was away visiting her kids and grandkids.

On Monday, Auntie Lin rang the doorbell again.

"The clay pot not good?"

Shobha sighed. "It's good but not good enough."

Her neighbour looked dejected, so she reassured, "Auntie Lin, I'll keep this. How much does it cost?"

"No, no," Auntie Lin refused and turned away.

In the evening, Subhash arrived with a strange look on his face. "Auntie Lin accosted me in the corridor, saying you want to visit India as soon as possible."

Shobha laughed so hard that tears streaked her cheeks. "I told her I can make the best curry only in an earthen pot, and I'll have to wait until I visit India."

"You are torturing her."

"What about the way she pesters me?" Shobha stood up in a huff. But she felt a twinge of guilt.

The next day, she set out early to get the best fish from the wet market. She cleaned the fish, sliced the shallots, washed the curry leaves, split the green chillies, and chopped the ginger and garlic. The Malabar tamarind was rinsed and ready.

Shobha waited for Auntie Lin as the fish curry simmered in the clay pot. But no one came.

She rang Auntie Lin's doorbell. No answer. She sent a message. The message was seen, but no one replied. She called the number, but no one attended.

Shobha spent an uneasy day until she received a call from Auntie Lin's son. "She was on the way to the market. A rash cyclist knocked her down. She's ok, but she needs to rest. I'll bring her home tomorrow."

Overcome with relief, Shobha thanked the universe.

Freshly prepared fish curry crossed the neighbourly threshold the next day. A smile broke out on Auntie Lin's face as she savoured a spoonful of the warm, spicy fish curry. "I'm so happy." She held Shobha's hand and confessed. "That day, I was cleaning cobwebs around the balcony. I reached out to sweep a corner and pushed your pot down."

Shobha gasped. "It was you?!"

Auntie Lin nodded.

"I feel so bad. You cannot make the curry. Now you can?"

"Can, lah!"

"The clay pot works?"

"The clay pot works," Shobha agreed with a grin.

THE QUEST FOR A FEAST

Maya looked at the message on her phone for the nth time after she left her apartment. The address remained unchanged. She had reached the right street, but the door number was nowhere to be found.

It was her seventh month in the city. Long enough to know how to get around, but too new to get acclimatized. It was also her first summer in the city. Summer at 18 degrees Celsius. Wearing a pair of gloves in summer looked silly. But she carried a pair in her pocket anyway. She winced as she blew on her cold fingers. The jacket could not be forsaken. Maya was not brave enough to wear summer clothes like the others on the bus.

The lure of good food pulled her halfway across the city on a train and onto another bus to reach this quiet, dainty-looking street. She covered the entire length of the street in ten minutes. Twice. Alone. Not a single soul on the grey asphalt with neatly trimmed hedges.

After the third time, Maya turned right into an alley. A convenience store. The unlikeliest place for the food that she yearned for. But her tummy fought hard with her heart, and after a few moments of deliberation, she dived into the store. She bought a cold sandwich. As cold as the wind playing around the trees.

The trees reminded her of home and made her miss the warmth. She trudged back into the street for the fourth time. But before she turned left, she spied a green expanse.

A park?

Turning to the right again, she came across a manicured piece of garden, open to the public. Seated on a comfortable bench, she munched on her sandwich. Hunger enhanced the taste, but her heart remained dissatisfied with every bite.

The last feast at home had been a stupendous success. Mom had whipped up many dishes, drawing herself into a frenzy and the guests into a post-lunch stupor.

Maya remembered seeing her mother sit by the kitchen table, savouring her own creations well past lunchtime. The guests snoozed on lounge chairs and chaises in the verandah while Maya clambered up to her room upstairs, only to find her bed occupied by cousins of various shapes and sizes, snoring away to glory. Maya had curled up on her grandfather's rocking chair, her breath keeping perfect time with the ups and downs of the gentle snores in the room.

As she took the last perfunctory bite of the bland sandwich, she tried to recollect the dishes from that day.

The sweet and sour concoction of tamarind and ginger awakened your taste buds, the crunchy nibbles kept you sane while the items were laid out on the banana leaf, the lemon pickle that lit a fire in your stomach, the fuchsia fantasy of a beetroot chutney, the orange sunshine of a pineapple gravy, the peaceable and passable green vegetable stir-fries, the browns and the whites, mixing morsel by morsel, a hint of a reality check with the bitter gourd, and, to top it all, the sweet proof of life in the pudding— everything served on a clean, green, and organic banana leaf.

Maya closed her eyes as she reminisced the magical moment when she would swipe the last morsel of the sweet payasam with a sleight of hand and a deftness that came with years of devouring the Sadya. Astonishingly, she heard the word in the background.

Sadya? A feast? Her eyes shot open, and she stood up at once.

A group of people staggered their way up the alley. She walked briskly like a woman on a mission. “Where’s the Sadya?”

One of the men pointed towards the convenience store. The others were too full to utter a word.

Maya ran to the convenience store. “Where’s the Sadya?” Maya yelled in exasperation.

The store clerk was startled like he had seen a crazy woman. He pointed to a door at the back.

Maya ran into the door, willing it to open by sheer mental power, but finally pushed through with both hands. She ran straight into a corridor at the end of another door. Pushing it open, Maya found herself amid a clean-up. She was shocked to see the neatly closed banana leaves. It was a sign that the food had been tasty and enjoyed sumptuously by the guests.

Two men with buckets and wiping rags in their hands stared back at her.

"Is it over?" her voice broke in dismay.

The men turned towards a third man who walked out of the kitchen. "We have enough to lay down one leaf. Why don't you take a seat?" he said.

Maya grinned. The two men smiled. The third man said, "Happy Onam!" She blessed them all.

THE POTBOILER

Ginger was in a daze. His ego hurt; he sat on the ground for a while before straightening his podgy legs to stand.

"Go back underground to your muddy mess!" The pungent words from Chiliram reverberated in the air.

Ginger tried to stand his ground, fighting back with equal pungency, if not more. "Don't be so vain and proud, Chiliram. Your flashy green coat will be gone before you know it."

But the smallest cell in his being knew that Chiliram could make the aficionados cry, hang their tongues, and wave their hands in hot exasperation. They still loved him because he added character to any bland potboiler, making it a blockbuster. Whereas Ginger, though handy, only singed their throats.

Chiliram never lost a chance to put him down. This morning was the worst because Jaggery stood nearby, and she saw everything. She was such a sweet girl. She did not deserve to see her beloved being ground down so hard.

Ginger decided that enough was enough. "Let's end this once and for all," he roared at Chiliram.

"Challenge accepted. But who would be the judge?"

"Let's decide in the court of oil. That will make our talents roil!"

Chiliram raised a green hand in acceptance.

Ginger bowed to the humble ground.

Jaggery came running to his side. “Ginger, don’t be such a fool. Chiliram has his own place in history. Why don’t you make peace with yours?”

“I am ready to be at peace, but Chiliram never stops pulling at my roots. I have to teach him a lesson.”

Jaggery shook her head in despair. “Listen, if you find yourself in trouble, just sizzle. I’ll be there by your side.”

Ginger clasped her hands with great care. “My dear Jaggery, do not worry. I would never dare to pull you into the court of oil.”

“But what if...?” Tears streamed down her crumbly dress, making it all stick together in allegiance.

“Wish me luck!” he said as he strode off to fight for his pride.

Meanwhile, Chiliram made all sorts of plans. He practised his moves, sharpened his tongue, and shook himself to raise his spice quotient. He had Tangy by his side. She promised to defend with all her tartness.

“Ginger can hold no flavour against us, Chiliram. Between us, we have what it takes to make mouths water.”

Chiliram nodded with a blooming pride. “Let’s go, Tangy. We have luck on our side.”

Off they went to the court of oil.

The waiting had induced a state of boil.

“Ginger! Ginger!” cried his fans from the stands.

“Chili! Chili!” yelled many on the other hand.

Ginger was the first to jump.

Jaggery gasped as oil changed his colours.

Chili gave a wry smile and jumped into the fray.

They battled it out until oil weakened their nerves. They seethed and trembled and shook with anger.

Chili looked pale and a mere shadow of himself. Ginger shrunk and shrivelled.

Tangy could control no longer, and she jumped into oil's battleground. The crowd cheered and clapped for her as she tried to save them both.

Jaggery took a deep breath and joined her friend.

The crowd went berserk, cheering and shouting with all their might.

Salt got too excited for his own good and soon found himself inside the court, a silent, dissolving spectator to the storm in the pot.

Mustard, Curry, and Fenu rushed to see the action up close, but their friends' frantic movements held them back. "If we join, it'll be a blockbuster," they all agreed. They watched as the court of oil turned dark and thick.

Soon, someone turned off the heat. The battle was done. The audience went home asking, "Who won?"

Someone yelled, "Everyone!"

The potboiler ended with a message, "Happy Onam!"

P.S. This story is an ode to the enigmatic side dish from Kerala, Puliyinji, usually prepared during festive occasions.

THE WRITERLY LIFE

"The object isn't to make art, it's to be in that wonderful state which makes art inevitable."

– Robert Henri

SOLITUDE

"How does one remove tea stains from the sofa?"

Madhu C R, the renowned author, typed into the Google search bar with an apprehension that rivalled that of a mechanic forced to investigate a legal case. When the results showed up, Madhu felt desperate, yet he smiled. Affection, followed by a smirk and a wistfulness, bubbled up as he thought of his daughter, son, and ex-wife in that order.

His daughter taught him that he could find anything on Google, his son scoffed at his complete sentences instead of 'keyword searches,' and his ex-wife knew everything, just like the website Google. It spewed so many results and options that he threw up his hands.

What should a man do to clean a patch of tea stain from his sofa? The soiled sofa cover did not bother him. But the splatter reminded Madhu of his ineptitude. He couldn't make his tea, nor could he clean his sofa.

It was four days since he spilled the tea and as many days since he had a sip. Madhu's Man Friday, Ali, hadn't knocked at the front door since he handed over the flask of tea last Monday.

Madhu scanned the landscape outside the square window in front of his desk. Not a soul in sight, which was not unusual. He was living alone on a hillock in a nondescript village nestled among the foothills of the Western Ghats of India.

Ten years ago, when he was looking for a place to enjoy a peaceful writing life, the only condition he put forth to the broker was that it should be a place where no one would know if he died. The broker had looked horrified, but he caught the drift. One winter morning, when Madhu was picking up the odds and bits from the Delhi apartment, the broker notified him that he had found the perfect location.

The estate and the modest house were a steal if Madhu was not bothered about the man whose stinking mortal remains were ignored in the woods behind the house until they attracted the local dogs. Madhu had expressed his subdued interest. Subdued, partly because he was shocked by how the broker took his stipulation literally and somewhat because the shift would further stretch the thin thread connecting him and his family.

The Delhi apartment was now his wife's. It used to be theirs. Madhu picked up his stuff or things he felt his wife wouldn't miss, wishing he could pick up his daughter as casually. But the court had ordered otherwise. He turned out to be an irresponsible father, an emotionally unavailable husband, and a mediocre writer. While the last flaw triggered the divorce, the first two mistakes strengthened the case.

Parenting and marriage appeared to be beyond redemption. At the new estate, where Madhu would be isolated, he sought solitude to redeem his writing talent.

Ali was the only intrusion that Madhu allowed in his isolated life. Ali took care of everything, cleaning the house, cooking, washing, and kitchen supplies, yet he spoke only when asked. "Distance brings people closer. You see, Madhu Sir, they will visit you soon," Ali commented within days of Madhu's arrival at the estate. Madhu's reminiscence of the days spent at Mussoorie with his two teenage children elicited his rare remark.

That was long ago. The teens were all grown up now. Ritu called him occasionally from her University at Oxford, where she taught a course in the Physical Sciences. Rakesh never contacted him, but Madhu heard about his exploits on Wall Street from Ritu. Smita had last called him five years ago for a property-related matter. Madhu himself did not make any attempt to connect. Despite such bleak prospects, Ali had offered an improbable dream of reconciliation.

"Where is Ali?" Madhu wondered. It was not just the house with its unclean floors, unwashed laundry, and desolate cold kitchen that missed Ali's presence. Madhu missed him, too. He had not read the newspaper since Ali disappeared because no one brought it for him.

There was something wrong, and he sensed it in his bones. Ritu had not called for over a month, but it was not just that. There was something else bothering Madhu. He did not use social media or own a TV set. He would have searched on Google had he known what to search. Something was happening in the world about which he wasn't aware. Something that he should know. It was like a sour taste at the back of his mouth, which refused to leave.

He picked up his mobile phone, a basic model that served his purpose: to receive calls from his agents and publisher or, at times, from Ritu. Ali was the only person Madhu ever called. But he had not attended Madhu's calls for the past four days.

Madhu scrolled through the few contacts on his phone, stopped at a name, and hesitated. He could ask her. She would know everything that was going on in this world. She might even know where Ali was, Madhu conjectured.

Smita knew everything about everyone. This quality had turned out to be a blessing and a bane for Madhu in the past. His debut as a writer was an accident, but he wasn't an accidental genius. He loved writing but had no flair for drama, humour, or any particular genre. He was working as an accountant at a publishing house, enjoying life as it may come.

He loved spending time with his family, especially his evening tea with his darling wife. Smita's stories about her relatives were hilarious and often brought him to tears. He started jotting them down in a diary. To Madhu's surprise, a publishing house colleague said the stories were terrific. He encouraged Madhu to write more. Either Smita had a vivid sense of imagination, or she knew a lot of interesting characters.

Madhu listened attentively to Smita whenever she spoke about a relative, family acquaintance, or friend. Slowly but surely, Madhu populated his diary with incidents and events that occurred in the lives of these characters.

After about a year, his colleague helped him secure a deal with a publishing company. Despite the lacklustre social media marketing and a lonely book launch event, the book was a roaring success.

Madhu was floating on cloud nine and dreamt of quitting his day job. That was before all hell broke loose. If he had known that the book would be a bestseller, he would have changed the characters' names in the book. But thanks to the sheer naivete of a first-time writer and the exuberant enthusiasm of his colleague who forgot to check with him, the book carried all the people's names from Smita's recollections verbatim. Calls, letters, and messages poured in from across the country, some even outside. Long-lost relatives expressed discomfort, anger, and disbelief at being a part of the book. On the one hand, Madhu's credibility as an author rose, but on the other hand, he lost his position in the extended family and the community.

Smita regretted not having read the draft when he asked her. She had dismissed her husband's writings as a mere excuse to lock himself up in a room. She wasn't even aware that the tales that she believed were entirely ignored by her husband had become the central theme of his writings. Madhu thought that she should have been happy about being his muse, at the least.

Smita's arguments against his impending writing life reached a crescendo one day when she said she wouldn't be surprised if he wrote about her and their kids.

"What clandestine secrets would I write about you three, Smita?"

"Aah, there is nothing to write about, I agree, but do you mean to imply that if there were, you would write about us?" Smita's eyes widened just like her mother's while making groundless accusations.

"I didn't mean to— "Madhu tried to reason.

"That's disgusting," Smita interjected, ignoring Madhu's protests.

The next time he saw her was with her luggage at the doorway. Their two kids, Ritu, twelve, and Rakesh, fourteen, stood beside her.

Five years of separation followed, during which he saw his kids only twenty times. An amicable divorce led to Smita getting ownership of the apartment. She knew all the right lawyers in the city and scratched up every flaw in Madhu's character.

Smita knew everything. Would she understand why he was suddenly feeling so paranoid? He dialled her number and waited for the high-pitched yet mellifluous voice to say hello.

"Hello? Long time. What's wrong?" Just like Smita to come straight to the point. She surmised that there was indeed something wrong.

"I don't know. I can't place it."

There was a long pause at the other end as if she had sucked in her breath and kept it inside, ready to blow it out if Madhu annoyed her more.

"Do you know Ali?"

"Who?"

"Ali, the guy who cares for the house, takes care of me. He has not turned up for the past four days."

"Did you try calling him?"

"Of course, I did. He did not pick up." Madhu hesitated before he expressed his doubts. "I have a bad feeling. That there's something wrong. Not just with Ali but with the world in general."

"Madhu, have you been reading the newspapers?"

"No. Ali used to bring them for me. Why?"

"Things are not all fine with the world, Madhu. There is a virus."

"A what?"

"A virus. It's spreading fast across the globe. Haven't you watched the news? God!"

"I came here to isolate myself, remember?"

"Doesn't mean you need to be under a rock, Madhu!"

Madhu disconnected after a few more pleasantries. So, there is a virus, but what has that got to do with Ali.

Madhu wandered into the kitchen and stood in front of the fridge. He could survive on biscuits or try to make tea, but he had run out of milk and biscuits. He had to step out of his self-imposed isolation and talk to people for which he hardly felt capable.

He gathered all his courage and will, most of which he had lost after his writing fiasco.

Walking down the rugged path outside the estate gate into the village below, he felt that the world was standing still. Not a soul was seen on the road, and the few that he spied were riding bicycles, hiding their faces behind masks, as if they were guilty of a shameful crime and hiding from humanity. He always thought hiding was good, so he held his handkerchief over his nose and mouth.

The sun shone straight and true onto his balding head, and he wished he had taken an umbrella. He wished he had stepped out before the sun decided to be so harsh. He wished Ali was around. He wished Smita had warned him about the umbrella and the sun.

Madhu longed for several things that were not there at that moment.

He walked unhurriedly but with purposeful steps towards the centre of the village. A masked policeman stood straight ahead. He waved his baton towards Madhu. "Sir, where are you going?"

Madhu smiled, painfully aware that other than Ali, this policeman was the first human he had met in years. He removed his handkerchief and said, "To the market to buy some milk."

"Where is your mask, sir? I could charge you a thousand rupees for not wearing it, you know?"

"Oh!" said Madhu and placed back his handkerchief.

"But why am I supposed to wear it?" Madhu asked in a muffled voice.

The policeman was near enough to tap him with his baton, which he did. "Sir, since you are a senior citizen, it is advisable that you stay at home instead of roaming outside."

"But I have no milk at home. No food."

The policeman proceeded to note down his address and his phone number. "We will take care of it."

Madhu looked all around him to see if there was anyone else around. Whom did he mean by 'we'?

The policeman pointed at the road behind Madhu. In a gentle but unwavering voice, he said, "Please go back home, Sir."

Madhu did not protest any further and returned. It did not occur to him that he should have asked the policeman about Ali. Perhaps he knew. Madhu turned to look at him. Like Smita, the policeman looked like someone who would know everything. But he waved Madhu away.

As night fell, Madhu heard the gate creak, and he peered out through the living room window. A tall man carrying bulging bags strode purposefully towards the main door. Madhu opened the door before the man could ring the bell. The man's eyes showed surprise, but it was difficult to tell whether he was pleased or angry as his face was hidden behind a mask.

"Sir, I've brought you some supplies. Let me know if you need anything else. Medicines, household stuff?"

Madhu recognised the voice. It was the policeman whom he had met in the afternoon. "That's very kind of you. Thank you."

"It's our duty."

Again, Madhu looked around appreciatively to see if there was a team of people who followed the policeman. But he was alone.

"Wait here. I'll get the money."

Madhu returned to the living room and took a box from a drawer. After paying the policeman, he examined the bag's contents. Not bad, he thought. The policeman had bought all the basic stuff an old man would need.

"Are you living alone too?" He wanted to ask the policeman, but he had already disappeared into the dark of the night.

He heated the milk and took two slices of bread from the packet the policeman had just brought. The bread and milk combo would be his dinner. Once he felt better, he realized he had not paid heed to Smita's words. He should check in on what's going on around him.

As he logged in to his computer, he was again reminded of his kids.

To Madhu, the computer symbolized his kids with their shiny new lives, fast-paced work, and the constant beseeching from his daughter to learn how to use Skype. He never liked the cold, steely box that pretended to be a portal to the world. He did not want a portal to the world. All he wanted to do was shut himself out of it.

Madhu sighed as he opened the only website he knew since his daughter spoke highly about it. He typed 'Virus' into the search bar, lo and behold. His screen was full of random, meaningless text; that's what he thought until he read it carefully. He learnt so much about viruses, especially the one racing across the globe on a fatal mission, that his head spun.

Madhu logged off from his computer and sat in horrified silence. People were getting sick, dying, isolated, and separated from their loved ones. He realized that he was isolated, too. The legal separation from Smita had cost him the apartment, which seemed like a small price for a life of solitude and peace. Ten years had gone by without hiccups, intrusions, or him stepping out of his house. When he stepped out, the empty street felt unfamiliar. The lone policeman appeared impassive, and the computer dumped a lot of unwanted information on him, leaving him untethered.

What if he were to die, and no one knew about it? Until the dogs came home following the stink. Would the policeman do the needful? Or would it be Ali? But where is Ali?

For the first time in ten years, Madhu felt helpless and lonely. He had enjoyed the solitude, but now he detested the isolation. He felt a panicky fear rising from the pit of his stomach to his chest, burning a hole in his heart. Madhu had to call his kids but didn't have an international calling facility. Calling Smita won't help. She would inhale deeply and wait for him to spell out what was bothering him.

The phone rang, and he saw Ritu's name flashing on the tiny screen. She had heard his thoughts from afar. "Hello? Pa?" Ritu sounded concerned.

"Yes, my dear."

"Are you alright? I read that there was a curfew in your area."

"I am alright. When can I see you, dear?" There was silence at the other end. "Hello? Ritu?"

"Pa, you've never asked me this before."

"Yes, I know. But I wish to meet you and Rakesh as well. Can you ask him to call me?"

"Pa, did you set up the Skype account?"

"No, I haven't. Is that necessary?"

"It will make calling and talking easier." Ritu drew a sharp breath, unlike her mom, who took a long time to breathe in. "Pa, we cannot travel anytime soon because of the pandemic. Neither me nor Rakesh. But we can see each other over Skype and talk to each other."

"Ok. Ok. I get it."

"Set it up by tomorrow, and I'll call at the same time to teach you how to make a call."

"Yes, dear. Thank you."

"Pa?"

"Yes, dear."

"Pa, solitude is a luxury, but isolation is not. It is forceful and desperate. People are isolated against their wishes but can do nothing about it."

"I understand."

"Write about them, Pa."

"I will, dear."

WRITING A BEST-SELLER

The bus lurched forward, forcing Yukta to grab the seat bar. Her pen dropped to the floor, and she caught her breath while she groped for it. The daily commute took a toll on her back.

Today was the rare lucky day when she found an empty seat. Despite the hectic and dull day at work, Yukta had a smile on her face. It was not just the seat that offered respite for thirty minutes in a one-hour commute but the interview that gave her a reason to be happy.

A famous author replied to her interview request. The author was well-known and had written more than a dozen books devoured by readers as soon as they were published. Her responses were witty, sharp, and to the point.

Yukta was composing an article for her blog. She knew her readers would love it.

She wanted to know her routine. The writer had a strict schedule.

Yukta had asked if she had a specific place to sit and write. The writer wrote about her retreat in the hills.

Yukta was mesmerised. She had read of writers who shut themselves up in rooms, who wrote inside reserved train compartments on long routes, and others who practically lived in the libraries. The writing life was so exciting. She nodded as she added her comments to her notebook.

A child screamed at the back of the bus. She read about the importance of family support, which the writer had emphasized in her response.

Yukta noted how family remained the fulcrum of every writer's existence. She felt proud of her choice of words.

A sudden uproar caused her to look out the window. The bus had nearly hit a couple travelling on a scooter. The building ahead looked familiar.

Gosh! She nearly missed her stop. She got up in a hurry, clutching her notebook and pen. The passengers pressed forward, ready to disembark, but the bus driver had to pacify the scooter couple before he could inch forward to the bus stop.

The bus stop was a few hundred metres away. Some passengers walked out in a huff. Yukta joined them and added to her daily step count.

She stopped by the vegetable market and recollected the writer's diet. "Nothing heavy during the day. I only eat food that keep my brain awake."

She stuffed her notebook and pen inside her backpack before carrying the heavy grocery bag. Covering the remaining kilometre on foot gave her time to think. The writer had emphasized daily exercise, yoga, and cardio, and now that she had crossed fifty, she added strength training. "I need my body to be physically fit so my brain works."

Yukta marvelled at the writer's focus. She was doing everything with the sole intent of maintaining the longevity of her writing life. Such determination!

Yukta reached home and went straight to the kitchen. A home-cooked meal was always the best, as the elders in the family would say.

While she cooked, she thought about what perspective she could add to the interview. The famous author had covered everything. Yukta needed more experience. She was only a blogger, not a published author or writer.

She enjoyed the rest of the evening with her family but brought out her notebook and laptop when everyone was asleep. The writer's interview motivated her. Yukta could only dream of such perseverance. If only she had half the talent and determination as the best-selling writer. As a first step, she would complete the blog post and add a few hundred words to her manuscript, a novel in progress. But first, she had to tackle her work emails.

A WRITER'S PARADISE

As the man watered the sole plant on his balcony, his neighbour called out. "Hello, Mr. David. I heard you move in yesterday."

David smiled in acknowledgement. "Yes, Good morning."

The neighbour waved bashfully as if dismissing a handshake that could not reach across the void between their blocks. "I am Roy."

David nodded and returned his attention to the plant.

Roy whistled a happy tune as he tended to his numerous flowerpots. Their blooming heads danced to his fingers as he patted and nursed them. "I love to see the colours. What are you growing?"

David gave an enigmatic smile but no reply.

Roy was miffed. Every morning, he would notice David giving inordinate attention to his unidentifiable wild plant while Roy beamed at his manicured shrubs and nourished flower beds. He whistled as he worked and ended his gardening hour with a smirk and a condescending nod at David's desolate little sapling.

Roy continued to holler a greeting every morning, which David acknowledged wordlessly with a nod and a smile. In a few days, it became clear that David had planted a wild vine. It extended its life betwixt the balcony grill. Roy would organise visits for his friends to 'ooh' and 'aah' over his plant children. They clicked pictures, posed among the blooms, and commented on his hard work and good fortune. Then they would cluck sympathies at David's lonely creeper. It had grown to cover half the grill but bore neither fruits nor flowers.

Roy arranged a coffee table and a couple of chairs on the balcony and enjoyed his morning and evening sips amidst his flowers. David rarely visited the balcony apart from spending a few minutes daily with his fantastical creeper, which now threatened to create a veil over the balcony grill.

As the creeper exhausted every iron bar, David offered a trellis for it to climb. Roy observed in confusion. Why was his neighbour allowing this wilderness to grow around him? He looked at his floral garden in satisfaction. Trimmed and maintained to perfection, his garden was the envy of all his neighbours, including David, he was sure.

One morning, Roy noticed that he could no longer see David. He wouldn't know if he was present on the balcony because the terrace and the trellis were entirely covered by the vine. Strange gardener! Roy thought as he eyed his chair. He hadn't sipped his tea in his garden for a long time. The flurry of visitors kept him busy.

Meanwhile, unlike before, David spent most of his time on the balcony. He sat at his desk in the middle of his wild and organic shed, away from prying eyes, condescending comments, and judgemental looks. The green roof towered above him as he nodded emphatically at his writer's paradise.

CO-EXISTENCE

A bee buzzed incessantly. The pen stopped in mid-sentence.

The writer gathered his stuff, cursed the noisy bee, and left the orchard with a foldable chair and a portable table in either hand, a flask over his shoulder, and a knapsack carrying two notebooks and a dozen pens. He lugged his writerly possessions across the town towards the nearby village.

Several other orchards dotted the village borders. The writer chose one lined with pomegranate trees under which he set up his writing table.

Alas! The lone bee disturbed him again.

The writer walked away from the orchard to a lake. He breathed in the moist air, gazed at the placid expanse, and found it most inspiring. The lake was the opposite of his mind right now— calm, composed, and a cooling presence. His mind wandered at a frenetic pace.

Was the bee in the orchard or inside his mind? Or was it a monkey prancing around?

The writer took a sip from his flask, commanded the monkey in his brain to sit quiet, and took up his pen. A group of young people gambolled across to the lake, their chatter and squeals creating an impression of a zoo.

The pen stopped mid-sentence again.

The writer sighed and gathered his things. He walked towards the mountains behind the village. He climbed to greater heights as the sun dipped towards the land. The rocks made his gait unstable. His possessions slowed him to an ungainly pace. But his thoughts soared with lithesome grace.

The writer set up the table and took a sip from his flask, but instead of picking up his pen, he lay down on the grey rocky ground under his feet. With his thoughts elevated and his mind grounded, he lay until he fell asleep.

In his dreams, he weaved a fantastic fable. The sentences blew in with the evening breeze while he picked the words from the rocky crevices. In the fable, the bee, the people, and the monkey co-existed in creative peace.

THE STORY OF A STORY

A story yawned upon a page.

It stretched into words and sentences, dug its prosaic roots into the whiteness, and put forth budding adjectives and blooming adverbs. Thoughts swooped down and rested on its branches. Memories climbed and curled up in its nooks and crannies. Worries took a nap under its shade.

The story grew in creeping paragraphs and leaping chapters into a tome of biblical proportions. Imagination ran riot inside the story while characters indulged in epic conversations.

A song weaved into the story, and the pictures danced to a new tune. But as the story grew in size, the gardener felt fear.

Fear of the unknown, the unexperienced, the unimaginable, and the inexplicable. She trimmed its branches, hid its roots, and plucked its leaves and blooms.

The thoughts flew away, the memories crawled back into the past, and the worries awoke in distress. The song weaved its way out, leaving the pictures in a huff.

Now, the story sits in a tiny corner of the garden, cut to size as per popular taste.

JOMO CALLS

AN EARTHY CAUSE

Parched earth and lips. The ground lay barren and cracked. The lips, barely moistened by a thirsty tongue, seared in the hot sun.

Patsy sunk down on the flat, unyielding land. The pebbles poked into his bare legs. He twisted his arms to open his backpack and hoped his muscles would yield despite dehydration. The steel water bottle was warm. He drank the water in measured sips. As per the map, he had six more kilometres before he hit the next village.

This one was a disaster.

Some say it's a climate disaster, others blame migration, few blame poor governance, and a handful call it destiny.

As far as Patsy was concerned, he didn't find anything worth his time or effort. It was one of those villages where the wad of notes in his shorts mattered to no one. Heck, he couldn't even fill his bottle.

The only watering hole on the way was swarming with thirsty animals and humans. There were tiny kids, too. Their parents, too insecure to leave them home for fear of missing out on the precious water, had posted them nearby under a makeshift tent.

The kids' sallow eyes watched his every move as he trudged toward the crowd.

Patsy couldn't bear to ask for his share from this rationed supply. He knew even money would not deter them from defending their only source of the elixir of life. He turned away, embarrassed and dejected.

Patsy had set out on this zealous route to find something genuine. He wished to invest his hard-earned money in a worthy cause. Patsy wanted to save the world. He couldn't even solve a water crisis of a few hundred people. A shame!

Trudging away from those oppressed villagers, he promised the universe he would return, though his sixty-year-old body raised compelling concerns.

A sudden cool breeze awakened his senses. Moist air. He squinted towards the distance. The breeze blew from the front, explaining why his face felt touched by an angel. He quickened his pace and forgot about his aching calf muscles. There was water somewhere. He could feel it.

In a few yards, the splintered ground began to heal. The mud stuck together like love. Patsy knew immediately that water was the adhesive. He nearly ran towards the green patch in the middle of nowhere. A man worked with patient hands amidst shrubs and bushes. He looked up and smiled.

"I need water," Patsy whispered hoarsely.

"Come," the man said simply.

Patsy followed him and was stunned. A reservoir the size of a modest school playground shone with resplendent water. He dunked his bottle into the cool liquid and quenched his thirst.

"How?" he asked the man, who looked at him quizzically. "Did you know that your neighbouring village and many others struggle for water?"

The man nodded. "I tried explaining to them the importance of water harvesting. They wouldn't listen."

"They'll listen now. Just show them what you've done," Patsy waved his arms around.

"They can't afford it."

Patsy smiled. "I'm here just for that— an earthy cause."

THE REFUGE

"Kevin Samuel!" The lady called with the confidence that came with years of being ensconced behind a window in an institute of higher learning.

Gerald jumped to the window and presented his admission letter.

"Sorry, Gerald, is it?" she asked without raising her eyes. Her hands typed at a frenetic pace.

He nodded in reply. "Kevin was my father."

Something in his personal details caught her eye. She looked up. "Kevin Samuel? Didn't he work at the library?"

Gerald nodded.

"What happened?" her words lost some of their clerical sternness.

"He had liver problems, and then the fever struck."

"I am sorry, Gerald," the lady met his eyes briefly before she continued typing.

Gerald's hand shook as he held out the money. Three days before his father was hospitalized, he called Gerald to his room and told him about the bank account in his name.

"After your mother left us, I kept saving a bit every month. She did not trust me to save enough for your education. I am glad I haven't let her down. The money is for your college."

As Gerald accepted the receipt through the window, he wondered if his father had a premonition that he would collapse amongst the bookshelves at his workplace three days later.

The lady attempted a weak smile and then hollered at the next student.

Gerald swiped the screen of his phone to check his emails. Some of his friends had updated him about their admissions. Many had sent him invites to connect on various social media websites. He was wary. His father had warned him to stay away from those when he gifted him the phone on his fifteenth birthday.

Again, Gerald wondered if his father's uncanny intuition had something to do with the gift. The country went into lockdown a few weeks later, and the smartphone proved handy for online classes. The camera was good, and Gerald was gradually developing his photography skills. He sent a few to his friends, who suggested a social media website where he should upload the photographs.

But his father's warning rang in his ears. Now that he was alone in the world, every decision and every action would carry the weight of his father's words.

Gerald's home, which used to be a refuge for father and son whenever they missed his mother, will now have to hold the fort for heavier reminiscences.

When he reached home, he found a man sitting on the narrow porch outside the front door.

"Jerry? I am your uncle. Kevin must have told you about me?"

Gerald blinked.

The man sighed. "Well, why would he? When the family opposed his marriage to that lower-caste girl, I was the only one who supported him. But he paid no heed to us and settled here. So far from his family."

Gerald's face turned red, partly from the hot afternoon sun and the rest from the stranger's words. He opened his mouth to say, get out of my house! But the man rushed forward to embrace him before he could speak.

Gerald lost his breath but found his bearings and pushed him away. "I'm busy," he said while unlocking the door.

Turning for one last stare, he shut the door in his uncle's face. He didn't have an uncle. If he had, his father would have told him.

Gerald plonked on his chair angrily and whipped out his phone. The suggestions from his friends kept growing by the day. He glanced at the wall where his father and mother gazed at him benignly. He was all alone in this world now. Who else could help him out if not friends? Even if virtual? He took up their suggestion and created a profile.

Gerald Kevin Samuel sounded like a middle-aged man. Jerry was not a good choice because he didn't want any more long-lost uncles and aunts showing up on his profile. He typed in his name as GK.

GK was alone in the real world, but now he found refuge in the virtual world.

A NEW FRIEND

The pillar was not wide enough to hide her. Tara crouched, stood straight, turned sideways, and gathered her bag to hold it close.

She tilted her head to peep around the pillar.

The group of men stood in the same place as before. They weren't familiar. It was strange to see GK surrounded by so many people. Were they his followers from social media?

She let out a slow breath as she straightened. How long before they disperse? It was the last day of their examinations. They might have some plans for the evening.

For a second, Tara was sure that she ought to speak to GK. After all, he was her only real friend. But no, GK would never understand. He would keep pestering her to leave her favourite Jomo and take up a job in town. Something that she could not. Not when all her memories of her parents and grandmother stretched like a protective cloak over the Jomo Mountain.

She peeped again. The group had not budged.

An impatient Tara turned away from the pillar and walked confidently in the opposite direction, praying that GK would be too busy to notice her.

She strained her ears to listen. No one called out. Was she expecting someone to call her name?

Tara bit her lip as she reached a junction. It was the perfect summer day to be out and about; instead, she had spent her day tackling a confusing question paper on plant metabolism. Her own metabolism worked overtime these days. Her brain had consumed what little she had eaten in the morning. She crossed over to a path she had never tried before. It was shaded and appealed to her tired, burning eyes.

The walk calmed her after the exciting attempt to avoid her friends, mostly GK. The universe seemed to have vowed to make all her loved ones vanish. Tara abhorred close relationships now. She didn't need any company. Her home high up in the mountains was her refuge. No one would bother her there. She will continue to harvest seasonal vegetables. Perhaps tutor the schoolkids, find odd jobs, and—

A series of yelps and barks broke her reverie.

Tara proceeded cautiously towards a clump of trees beyond which she sensed the excitement. A blur of white, black, and brown fur and wagging tails greeted her at the turning. A rambunctious group of dogs of all sizes. Their leashes were tangled together in the hands of a laughing couple.

"We are sorry! They seem to be in a mischievous mood today!"

Tara stood aside respectfully while the group gambolled to a freshly cut lawn on the other side of the road. She smiled and chuckled with the group, feeling light and happy after a long time.

The group had bounded out from a house that said, "Nat and Freddie's Dog Shelter."

A whine escaped from the chinks below the closed front door, followed by a squeaky yelp and a scratching, like a kitten sharpening her claws against the wooden frame. Tara tip-toed, afraid that she might frighten the tiny creature on the other side. With a gentle nudge, she opened the wooden door.

Out bolted a dirty white ball of fur, and before she could figure out what happened, it had reached the road through the open gates. It wasn't a busy street, but vehicles occasionally drove on this stretch. Tara ran after it anxiously.

To Tara's relief, the furry bundle of enthusiasm stopped by the gate to investigate. The tail moved at sixty wags per minute, and the nose sniffed the grass like a detective sniffing out a case. She picked him up, and he immediately snuggled up to her.

"He likes you," said one-half of the couple who earlier crossed with the dogs. "Hi! I am Nat."

Tara glanced at the board. "Freddie is my husband," Nat added, nodding.

"Would you like to take him home? We found him on our doorstep yesterday. He loves to be held. Look how he snuggles in your arms. I think he is an orphan."

The word orphan cracked like a whip. Tara jumped. "I'll take him."

"Good! Think of a nice little name for this bundle of joy," Nat said as she ruffled his fur.

"Coco."

"Coco," Nat crooned, "looks like you have a new friend."

ACKNOWLEDGEMENTS

This compilation resulted from a year-long weekend exercise where I posted a short story on my Substack blog, ScubeStoryBasket.

I owe it to my family, my husband, Samoj, and my daughter, Samidha, for consistently sharing the pain and joy of writing. They continue to tolerate my Friday writing jitters.

I thank my parents and parents-in-law, who have always encouraged me to write, but more so because they saw my happiness in a seemingly unending writing practise. Having them in my life is my privilege, as they understand the process of chasing excellence.

I am genuinely grateful for my regular readers and commenters, the community I found on X (previously known as Twitter), and my Substack subscribers, who motivate me by reading my stories.

Special thanks to Louvina Andrade, Hemanth Sir, Vikram Chandrashekhar, Vikas Gaur, and Ramki, who graciously accept my tags on X whenever I post a new story.

www.ingramcontent.com/pod-product-compliance
Lightning Source LLC
LaVergne TN
LVHW041200150826
845673LV00001B/227

* 9 7 9 8 8 9 4 7 5 9 6 9 2 *